What I Want

A Stand-Alone Companion Novel
to the *Chop, Chop* Series

L.N. Cronk

Edited by Barbie Halaby

Published by Rivulet Publishing
West Jefferson, NC, 28694, U.S.A.

This book is dedicated to each person who has read the entire *Chop, Chop* series and is still coming back for more. I am so thankful for each of you ~ many blessings!

I urge, then, first of all, that petitions, prayers, intercession and thanksgiving be made for all people – for kings and all those in authority, that we may live peaceful and quiet lives in all godliness and holiness. This is good, and pleases God our Savior, who wants all people to be saved and to come to a knowledge of the truth. 1 Timothy 2:1–4

Author's Note:

Despite the way this story is written, many of the conversations at the beginning of this book – especially those with Bizzy – would actually have been spoken in Spanish. While I'm sure my great friend Vicki Krueger would have been willing to translate for me as she always has (thank you, Vicki!), using so much Spanish dialogue would have significantly distracted from the novel. Therefore, for the sake of the story, only a few lines of Spanish are actually included.

I hope you enjoy it ~ many blessings to you!
L.N. Cronk

~ ~ ~

Feisímo.

My entire life, people have called me this.

Most often, my sister Grace – hissing it into my ear whenever she thought she could get away with it. Other times it was my classmates, counting on their words to be drowned out by the noise of other children on the playground during recess. Sometimes it would be a little kid at a restaurant, blurting out the truth before a mortified parent could shush them into silence. Occasionally it might be a stranger on the street, not actually saying anything, but glancing away in embarrassment for me, saying it all the same, even without any words.

Throughout the years, many different people have told me in many different ways, and despite my parents' constant attempts to convince me otherwise, I know exactly what I am . . . what I've always been.

I have always known.

Feisímo . . .

Ugly as sin.

~ ~ ~

FIRST OF ALL, let me make it perfectly clear that it wasn't just because she's blind that Bizzy and I got together.

I'll admit that it helped . . . I never would have gotten up the nerve to even *talk* to Bizzy on my own if she'd been able to see what I looked like right off.

I'd seen a movie one time with a blind person feeling somebody's face so they could "see" what that person looked like with their sense of touch. So the first time I laid eyes on Bizzy, I immediately reached my hand to my upper lip and felt my scar, trying to determine what it would feel like to her if I ever let her touch my face.

I decided that it didn't feel as bad as it looked.

I was born with a cleft palate. Not just a hare lip or something, mind you, but a *severe* cleft palate. Go right now to your nearest search engine and type in "complete bilateral cleft." Pick out the worst picture you see. That was me.

I'm nothing like that anymore of course. I've had reconstructive surgeries, and if you saw me you might not notice the scar and the asymmetry of my nose and lip right away . . .

What you'd notice right away is my hands.

Now type into your search engine "symbrachydactyly." Find a picture of a pair of hands that look pretty normal, but with no fingers – just little nubs.

I didn't have reconstructive surgery for that.

And by the way, I absolutely hate that word. *Nubs*. I wouldn't use it if I didn't have to, but sometimes I don't have a choice.

Anyway, I do actually have one finger . . . a thumb really. It's not a great thumb, but it's all I've got. And if it sounds like I feel really sorry for myself, I want you to know that I don't. Not at all. I don't wish anything was any different about any part of my life. Everything that has ever happened to me has made me who I am today, and I wouldn't have it any other way. And I really like my thumb . . . it comes in very handy.

So, anyhow, after I felt my scar, I thought about my hands. I thought about how Bizzy was bound to find out about them eventually, but that since she was blind she might actually get to know me a little bit *first* . . . before she found out.

That intrigued me.

And so, as soon as I saw Bizzy that very first day and thought about all this, I decided to go for it.

For some reason, despite the way I look, I had never really doubted that there was someone out there for me. I had also always known that the person I was going to end up with one day would probably have something wrong with them, but it had never occurred to me that the "something" wrong with them might be that they were blind.

Deformed is what I had always imagined actually . . . another person like myself. Someone better suited for the Island of Misfit Toys.

But Bizzy wasn't deformed at all. She was pretty. Her hair was black and shiny and her skin was smooth and clear and her smile was the prettiest I'd ever seen. The only thing wrong with her was that her pupils were milky white instead of black . . . and someone like me had no right to complain about something like that.

The day I first met Bizzy, Grace and I had walked from school to the orphanage. Our mom worked there and it was where we had practically grown up, spending hours of our free time helping out with things or playing with the orphans.

My least favorite job at the orphanage was doing the dishes. The plates and cups and silverware just had to be rinsed off and run through this automated thing, but the pots and pans had to be washed by hand in a sink with disgusting bits of food floating around in it and I hated that.

Volunteering to take Grace's place at the sink probably wasn't the smartest move I'd ever made since it immediately made her suspicious, but I did it anyway because I needed a good excuse not to have to shake hands with Bizzy right away (should she decide that she wanted to). Grace went off with a perplexed look on her face after I shoved my hands into the dishwater and started furiously scrubbing a bread pan.

"Hi," I said to Bizzy, who was standing in front of the rinse sink. "My name's Marco."

"Hi, Marco." She smiled. "I'm Isabelita, but everybody calls me Bizzy."

"They didn't waste any time putting you to work," I noted as I set the pan into her sink so she could spray it off.

"No," she agreed as she rinsed. "I guess it's better just to jump right in to everything."

"Where are you from?" I asked.

"Villa de Paz."

Villa de Paz was another orphanage on the other side of Mexico City. Sometimes, when their funding was running low, they would send kids to our orphanage.

"How long have you lived here?" she asked, setting the pan on the drain board.

"I don't," I said. "My mom works here."

"Oh . . . are you Grace's brother?"

"Um-hmm," I admitted, hoping I didn't sound too sour about it.

"I just met her," Bizzy said. "She seems really nice."

I rolled my eyes. Yeah. I'm sure she *seemed* really nice . . .

We chatted through the rest of the pots and pans, and I told her all about how I was the youngest of six children and how all of us had been adopted – Doroteo and Lily and I right from this very orphanage in Mexico. Doroteo, who we called Dorito, was my only brother. Amber, Meredith, and Grace were half-sisters and had been born in the United States, where my parents were originally from. Dorito had just gotten married. Amber and Lily were attending college in the States.

4

Bizzy told me that her parents had given her up as soon as they'd discovered she was blind, and she told me that she'd lived in one orphanage or another for her entire life.

In my opinion, it's hard to turn out normal when you're not only handicapped, but you've been abandoned, too. I was turning out pretty good (if I do say so myself), but that was only because my parents were exceptional people. If it weren't for them, I can't even imagine where I'd be.

So with that in mind, looking back, I think that one of the things that amazed me the most about Bizzy was how normal she was. She was blind, and she was an orphan, but she was brilliant and friendly and happy and fun and full of life and self-confidence . . .

And I was always really glad that I'd decided to do the dishes that day.

It's possible that Grace saw the same things in Bizzy that I did and simply wanted her for a friend, but it's also entirely possible that Grace just realized that I liked Bizzy and she couldn't stand the thought of me having something she didn't have for even one teeny, tiny second. Whatever the reason, Grace's friendship with Bizzy grew as fast as mine did, and if Grace hadn't had gymnastics two days a week after school, I never would have had any time alone with Bizzy at all.

It was on one of my "alone" days with Bizzy that I decided I'd better tell her what I looked like because on TV shows and stuff, people always keep secrets over some little thing and then it winds up turning into a big, huge thing and they always end up with all sorts of problems that could have been avoided if they'd been honest right from the get-go. Bizzy and I had been spending time together every day for two weeks, and her first impressions of me were long gone. Either she liked me or she didn't (and I was kind of thinking that maybe she did), but no matter what, I knew that she wasn't the kind of person who was going to change how she felt about me just because she found out what I looked like. On the other hand, though, she might be really hurt if she found out that I'd been dishonest with her.

Two weeks was pretty much the borderline between, "Oh, it just hasn't come up yet," and "Oh, I've pretty much been keeping a secret from you."

And so, on gymnastics day, I asked Bizzy if she wanted to go out front and sit on the steps.

"The sun feels good," Bizzy said, turning her face toward it once we got outside.

"Yeah," I agreed.

We sat quietly for a moment until I got up the nerve to break the silence.

"I want to tell you something," I finally said.

"What's that?" she asked, turning her face from the sun to me instead.

"I . . . I want you to know something about me," I said.

"Okay."

"There . . . there were some things wrong with me when I was born," I began. "I don't look like everyone else."

"You mean your hands?" she asked.

"How did you know about that?" I asked, dumbfounded.

"Grace told me," she said, shrugging. "She told me about your cleft palate, too."

"She did," I said flatly.

"Yes." Bizzy nodded.

I *hated* Grace.

"Why didn't you tell me?" I asked.

"I didn't want to make you self-conscious or anything," she explained, shrugging again. "I figured you'd tell me when you wanted to."

"Oh."

And that was when I suddenly realized that Bizzy had been purposely avoiding my hands for two weeks whenever I'd offered her my arm to guide her someplace. Until then, I'd just thought that I'd gotten incredibly lucky.

"Are you mad at me because I knew and didn't say anything?" she asked.

"No," I said. "Are you mad at me because I didn't tell you before now?"

"No," she said with a smile.

"Do you want to feel my face?" I asked her.

"What?"

"You know," I said. "So you can see what I look like?"

"That's not going to help me know what you look like," she laughed.

"It's not?"

"No," she said. "Where'd you get that from? Some movie?"

I bit my lip.

"Blind people don't go around feeling other people's faces," she explained with another laugh. "Just tell me what you look like."

"Apparently Grace already told you."

"Not really," Bizzy said. "I want you to tell me."

"Well, I've got this really bad scar where they closed up the gap between my nose and my mouth and my hands don't really have any fingers, just these little . . ." – I sighed inwardly – "these little *nubs* that are kind of webbed together."

I paused and waited for her reaction.

"No," she said, giving me a big smile. "I mean tell me what you look like. What color is your hair and everything?"

"Oh," I said. "Well, my hair is dark and wavy and I keep trying to grow it longer and my dad keeps making me get it cut. I have really dark brown eyes and I'm fairly tall for my age. I'm skinny . . . too skinny. My mom says I should quit complaining about that."

She smiled again.

"What about your skin?" she asked.

"Well," I said. "I'm Latino like you. My skin's a lot like yours."

"I don't really know what I look like," she reminded me.

"Oh," I said. "Right."

"Will you tell me?"

"What?"

"Tell me what I look like."

"Oh," I said again. "Well, umm, you're Latino . . ."

She laughed.

"And your skin is fairly light. It's like butterscotch and it looks really smooth and soft."

She gave me yet another smile.

"And you have the prettiest smile I've ever seen," I told her.

"What about my eyes?" she asked.

"They're dark brown," I said. "Like mine."

"Do they look like everyone else's?" she asked.

I hesitated for a moment. Was it possible that in thirteen years, no one ever told her what her eyes looked like?

"No," I said finally. "Most people have black pupils. Yours are white."

She seemed to be taking that in as she sat quietly for a moment.

"You're very pretty," I told her. She smiled again, but it didn't seem like her heart was in it this time.

"Do you want to go in and play rummy?" she asked.

Bizzy had a braille card deck and killer instincts. She was a lot of fun to play cards with.

"Sure," I agreed. "But I'm gonna beat you this time."

The next day, when Grace and I arrived at the orphanage after school, Bizzy was wearing sunglasses.

"Cool shades," Grace told her, but as soon as I had the chance, I pulled Bizzy aside and asked her why she had them on.

"I wear them sometimes," she said, shrugging.

"No, you don't," I argued. "You've been here for over two weeks and you haven't worn them once. The only reason you have them on is because of what I told you yesterday."

"I just want to look pretty."

"You *do* look pretty," I said. "I already told you that you're pretty."

"Well, then," she said, shrugging again slightly, "I want to look even prettier."

"These don't make you look prettier," I told her, reaching to gently take them off.

She didn't answer.

"When you smile," I said, "it lights up your whole face. All these do is cover half of that up."

She still didn't say anything.

"Don't wear these," I said. "If you want to be prettier, just smile even more."

"Okay," she said, and she did.

Bizzy didn't wear her sunglasses anymore after that, but I always felt really guilty that she'd ever put them on in the first place. The very last thing I had ever wanted to do was to make Bizzy feel for even one small second the way I had felt for my entire life.

A few weeks later, Mom let me and Grace have Bizzy come over for dinner one evening. Of course Grace monopolized her like always, but during the meal, Dad asked us about our homework and found out that Grace still had algebra to do. After that, I got Bizzy all to myself for a bit while Grace and Dad fought about math.

I took Bizzy around the house, describing everything to her that she couldn't see, and eventually we ended up in my bedroom.

"What's that noise?" she asked.

"What noise?"

"It sounds like water," she said. "And a motor."

"Oh," I said, nodding even though she couldn't see me. "That's my fish tank."

"You have fish?"

"Yeah," I said. "Guppies."

"Guppies," she repeated.

"Yeah," I said again. "Fancy guppies. They're live breeders. One of them had a bunch of babies yesterday."

"Really?" Her entire face lit up.

"Uh-huh."

"What do they look like?" she asked.

"They're really little," I answered. "They're basically see-through bodies with eyes."

"Oh," she said wistfully. "I wish I could see them."

"You can hold one if you want," I offered.

"Really?"

"Yeah."

"It won't hurt it?"

"I don't think so," I answered. Actually I was worried that this might not be such a great idea and I didn't really want anything to happen to one of my guppies, but I decided that I wanted to see Bizzy smile even more.

"Okay," she said, excitement growing in her voice.

I got out my net and ran it through the water, catching several babies. I pulled the net out of the water and held it over the tank, turning it inside out and carefully getting one of the babies onto my hand. I reached for one of Bizzy's hands and gently put the baby guppy onto the end of her finger.

"Can you feel it?" I asked.

"That's a *fish*?" she asked in awe.

"Yeah."

"I can't believe how small it is!"

"I told you they were little."

Carefully, Bizzy brought her thumb to her finger so that the guppy was lightly caught between them. She held it for a moment, her face glowing.

"I want to put him back now," she said after a minute. "I don't want to hurt him."

"Okay," I agreed, and I guided her hand to the tank, dipping her finger into the water.

"Is he okay?" she asked worriedly.

I looked at him. He floated on his side for a moment and then righted himself. He sat motionless for another second before darting off toward the heater.

"He's fine," I told her, and she broke into a big grin.

I looked at her smile. I loved that smile.

I still had hold of Bizzy's hand. I kept holding it and continued looking at her, and slowly her smile started to fade. Not as if she wasn't happy anymore, but as if she knew that I was looking at her and as if she knew exactly why.

I didn't say anything, but I moved closer, knowing she could tell. I watched her face to see her reaction.

10

And her reaction was that she closed her eyes.

I hesitated, but only for a second longer. I leaned closer still and kissed her lightly, hoping desperately that my lip wasn't so messed up that she could tell and hoping that I was doing it right and . . .

What I *should* have been hoping was that Grace wouldn't pick that very moment to come traipsing down the hall.

I heard her gasp and Bizzy and I quickly pulled apart from each other. I turned toward the door, mortified.

Grace gaped at me with her mouth open for a second but then quickly pulled herself together, a nasty grin spreading across her face. She turned on her heel and started back down the hall. Immediately, I took off after her.

"Don't," I said after I'd caught up with her and grabbed her by the arm.

"Don't what?" she asked innocently.

"Don't screw this up for me," I pleaded quietly. "Please don't."

"You don't need me to screw it up for you," she said, the grin returning to her face. "I'm sure you'll do that all by yourself." And then she yanked herself free from my grasp and continued down the hall.

I watched after her as she disappeared around the corner. Getting inside my head was one of Grace's specialties, but I wasn't going to let her do that to me this time . . . I was *not* going to screw this up.

I headed back to my room.

"I'm sorry," I said as soon as I was in front of Bizzy again.

"For what?"

"Umm," I hesitated. "For anything you might possibly be upset about right now?"

She laughed. "I'm not upset about anything."

"You're not?"

"No," she said, shaking her head and smiling at me again.

"Good," I said, and I hoped that she could hear in my voice that I was smiling too.

Grace and I both rode along when my mom took Bizzy back to the orphanage that evening, and Bizzy told Mom that I'd let her hold a baby guppy. She didn't mention anything about kissing.

"I love animals," Bizzy said. Then she added longingly, "I would love to have a pet."

"Have you ever thought about getting a Seeing Eye dog?" my mother asked her.

"Yes," she said, "but there's a lot to it."

"Like what?" Grace asked.

"Paperwork and travel and you have to get trained how to handle them properly and it . . . it's just not real easy."

She didn't say it, but I knew that what she meant was that it wasn't real easy when you're an *orphan*. Not real easy when you don't have a mom and a dad to help you and make it all happen.

It made me sad to think that Bizzy was never going to have what I had. No family to take her on vacations. No one to tell her stories about all the cute, funny things she'd done when she was a little kid. No house to live in so that she could own a pet. I found myself wishing that there was a way I could help Bizzy to have everything that she was missing . . . everything that I already had.

When we arrived at the orphanage, we walked with Bizzy into the building, and Mom went to go talk to the director while Grace and Bizzy and I hung around in the commons area. Grace and Bizzy were carrying most of the conversation, but whenever Grace wasn't talking, she was pursing her lips at me, closing her eyes, and making silent, exaggerated kissing motions in the air.

Once Mom was finally ready to go, we all said goodbye to Bizzy and headed out to the car. We'd barely made it out the door though when Mom suddenly remembered that she had one more thing to take care of. She turned and went back into the building, promising to be right back out. Grace and I continued on to the car.

I got there before she did and took the front seat. As soon as Grace climbed into the back, I turned around and started pounding her as hard as I could. She pounded right back until she saw Mom coming, and then both of us sat down and I faced forward, crossing my arms.

Neither of us said a word.

"What's going on?" Mom finally asked after we'd ridden along for a while in silence. It wasn't unusual for Grace and me to not talk to each other, but usually we at least talked to her.

"Nothing," I said.

But at that same exact moment, Grace blurted out, "Marco and Bizzy were *kissing!*"

"Shut up!" I yelled, undoing my seatbelt. I turned around and climbed halfway over the seat, starting to pound on her again.

Mom caught me and forced me back down, ordering me to put my seatbelt back on while Grace continued.

"They were in his bedroom," she said. "And they were all like 'oohhh . . . mmhhhmm'." She started kissing at the air like she'd done earlier, but this time not so silently.

"Shut UP!" I yelled at her again.

"Grace," my mom said wearily. "I want you to leave your brother alone."

Having six kids, Mom knew exactly how to handle kissing teenagers, but none of our other siblings had ever fought like Grace and I did. Mom still didn't have a clue how to deal with the two of us.

I crossed my arms in front of me again while Grace ignored her, calling out in a singsong voice, "Mar-co's got a *girl-friend.*"

"Grace," Mom said, now using her warning voice. "Apologize to your brother."

"Sorry," Grace said. I didn't look back at her, but I could tell from the way she said it that she had a big grin on her face.

"Marco," Mom said. "Tell your sister you forgive her."

"Whatever," I muttered.

Mom sighed again and didn't push it.

I kept my eyes straight ahead, keeping my arms crossed and trying to act upset, but in reality I could barely suppress the happiness that was welling up inside.

I wondered about what Grace had just said, and the more I thought about it, the happier I felt. I crossed my arms even tighter, like I was trying to hold everything inside of me so that I could savor it forever.

Had Grace really meant what she'd just said? And, if so, was it true?

Did I actually have a girlfriend?

~ ~ ~

AS IT TURNS out, I actually *did* have a girlfriend – and I bent over backward to make sure that I didn't screw things up like Grace had assured me I would. I made sure that I never did anything wrong and I did whatever I could think of to make Bizzy happy so she wouldn't break up with me.

I wrote her notes while I was at school and read them to her when I met her at the orphanage in the afternoons, and I collected romantic songs and played them for her, telling her why they made me think of her. If I ever saw a dog while we were out walking, I would always try to get Bizzy close so that she could pet it, and I would watch her face light up as she stroked its fur. I took her to the movies and spent my time in the darkness leaned in close so that I could whisper in her ear what was happening and enjoy the sensation of her hair and skin against my lips. I baked her peanut butter cookies because they were her favorite, and I never bad-mouthed Grace to her because Bizzy told us both that she didn't want to hear it.

I treated Bizzy like gold.

Bizzy's birthday was on a Saturday at the beginning of October. On that day, I headed over to the orphanage as soon as I'd scarfed down some breakfast and emptied all the trashcans like Mom had told me to.

I invited Bizzy to go to the park with me, and when we arrived, we sat on a bench together and I handed her a small cardboard box. She opened it carefully, lifting the lid and tentatively fingering the little objects that lay on top of the thin layer of cotton. She furrowed her brow in obvious confusion.

"What are these?" she asked.

"Jumping beans."

Her brow knit together even tighter as she picked one up, feeling it deliberately.

"What's that?" she asked, running a finger over two little bumps she found.

"It's supposed to be braille," I explained as she picked up another one.

"You *carved* these?" she asked in surprise.

"I tried."

It had taken me a long time to make a different braille letter on each bean (and I'd killed plenty before I finally succeeded – cutting too deeply and exposing the writhing white larva inside whenever I did). When I was finished, however, I had nine of them, and I watched now as Bizzy felt each one and her face lit up. Slowly she laid them out before her on the bench:

I . . . S . . . A . . . B . . . E . . . L . . . I . . . T . . . A

"I wanted you to have some kind of a pet," I explained as the "S" gave a little jump.

"That's so sweet," she said, giving me one of those smiles that I loved so much. Then I leaned forward and she let me give her one of those kisses that I loved so much too.

A few weeks later I knocked on Grace's door – not something I usually did unless I had to.

No answer.

I knocked again.

Still no answer.

Finally I banged as hard as I could and she yelled that it was unlocked, so I tentatively opened her door and stuck my head inside her room.

Grace was lying on her back, reading, with earbuds stuffed in her ears and music blaring so loud that I could tell what song it was from ten feet away. Mom and Dad were always getting on

16

her about listening to her music so loud (and since our older sister Lily was completely deaf, you'd think that Grace would have had a little more sense about something like that, but of course she didn't).

"What do *you* want?" she asked when she realized who had been knocking, her voice full of disdain.

I didn't answer.

When she finally grasped that I wasn't going to talk until she could hear me, she rolled her eyes dramatically and pulled out one of her earbuds.

"What?"

"I need your help," I said.

That caught her attention. She pulled out the other earbud, not wanting to miss the sound of opportunity knocking.

"What?"

"I want to buy Bizzy a violin for Christmas," I said. "Mom and Dad said they'll pay half, but I have to pay the other half."

Bizzy had told us both how much she loved the violin and had wistfully mentioned on more than one occasion that her dream was to play professionally. If I could pull this off, I was fairly certain I'd be her hero forever.

"If you help pay for it," I promised Grace, "it can be from both of us."

Grace narrowed her eyes, obviously considering my proposition. Even though she was a total jerk to me, I knew that she wanted Bizzy to have something nice just as much as I did.

She thought for another moment.

"How much?" she eventually asked.

"The whole thing is three-fifty."

"New?"

"No."

"Where'd you find it?"

"Máximo's."

"How do you know it's any good?"

"He played it," I said. "It sounded good."

"Like you know what a good violin sounds like," she scoffed.

"You know what?" I said, starting to turn around. "Just forget it. I'll give it to her by myself."

"No. No," she said hastily. "Wait."

I turned back and looked at her expectantly.

"So," she said, calculating hard. "Eighty-seven fifty?"

Genius.

I nodded.

"Okay," she decided. "But it's from both of us and I get to be there when she opens it."

"Deal."

Grace already had some money saved from babysitting and stuff, so when she got Mom to agree to pay her for washing all the windows and screens in the entire house, it took care of the rest of what she needed.

I, on the other hand, was completely broke, and I had to pester Mom and Dad constantly to let me do work around the house so that I could earn extra money. I mulched, I trimmed, I detailed the car, I wiped down all the cupboards in the kitchen, and I moved every single piece of furniture in the house so that I could vacuum underneath.

I think they both got pretty tired of trying to think up things for me to do because when I tried to convince Mom that she needed to pay me to wash and refold all the clean sheets and towels in the linen closet, she talked with the director at the orphanage and arranged for me to do some odd jobs there instead. The orphanage wasn't exactly in a position of paying kids to do extra work, so I'm pretty sure that Mom was actually the one who was paying me, but I didn't really care where the money came from. All I worried about was having enough money to buy that violin for Bizzy, and by the time Christmas arrived, I did.

Mom let us have Bizzy over for dinner on Christmas Eve. When Grace handed her the violin, I think she knew what it was right away, even though it was in a box.

She pulled off the wrapping paper and opened it, slowly drawing the bow out first and then running her delicate fingers over the violin, a look of disbelief on her face.

"This is for me?" she asked, awe in her voice.

"Yes," I said. "It's from me and Grace."

"Go on," Grace urged her. "Try it."

Bizzy still looked a bit like she was in shock, but she gave Grace a nod and lifted the violin to her chin. She raised the bow and dragged it across the strings, stopping a time or two to twist the tuning pegs, and as the violin emitted its first few squeaks and squalls, I was suddenly struck with an awful thought.

What if she was terrible? What if she couldn't play at all?

Soon, however, Bizzy stopped tuning and took a deep breath. She closed her eyes, raised an elbow high, and effortlessly ran the bow over the strings. It only took about two notes for my fears to be completely assuaged.

Have you ever had one of those moments where your heart is so full of joy that it feels like it's swelling inside your chest and it's all you can do to hold back the tears but you don't really even know why?

That's how I felt right then, listening to Bizzy play.

Christmas Eve pretty much made me feel like that anyway. When I was little, I would sneak out of my bedroom after everyone else was asleep and plug in the lights to the tree. I would sit on the floor in the darkened living room and stare at the glimmering lights until Dad came out and found me and scooped me up. He would carry me back to bed, holding me tight and whispering into my ear that Santa was going to take back my presents and give me coal instead. I would giggle quietly against him, not believing him for a second. Everything was too right in the world for that to ever happen.

That was how I felt right now . . . like everything was right with the world. She played "What Child Is This?" and it was absolutely beautiful.

Everything was beautiful.

Bizzy was beautiful . . . my parents were beautiful . . . my life was beautiful . . .

I looked at Grace.

Even *she* was beautiful.

Grace glanced at me, as if she sensed I was looking at her, and I felt myself smile at her.

And like a Christmas miracle, she smiled back. It was as though she knew that we had done something truly wonderful by working together and as if things were finally going to be okay between the two of us.

Suddenly I was glad she was in my life . . . glad that she was my sister.

Bizzy finished playing and lowered her new violin, turning her face toward me and Grace again.

"Thank you," she told us both softly, tears filling her eyes. "I can't believe you did this for me."

"You're welcome," Grace said, turning to look at her and still smiling. "It was my idea."

Bizzy and her violin were a big hit at the orphanage. Most days when I arrived there after school that winter and spring, Bizzy would already have five or six little kids hanging around her, begging her to play something for them. She usually obliged and even started going on the Internet to listen to various songs that they requested. It always amazed me how she could listen to a song and then turn right around and play it by ear, seemingly without a mistake. But Bizzy insisted that she made *plenty* of mistakes.

"Not that I can tell," I said.

"I need lessons," she complained.

"Don't you take lessons at school?" I asked. (Bizzy went to a public school – I went to a private one.)

"*Real* lessons," she said. "I need real lessons." And for the millionth time, I wished that I could give her everything that she wanted.

I may have wished I could give Bizzy everything that she wanted, but that's not the same as wishing that Bizzy *had* everything she wanted.

I wanted to be the one to make her happy so that I would get credit. I wanted her to love me and need me the way that I loved her and needed her. If all I'd wanted was for Bizzy to be truly happy, I would have wanted for her what happened next.

~ ~ ~

SUMMER VACATION WAS just around the corner. I was going to a couple of soccer camps, one math camp, and one quick trip to the States, but other than that my summer was pretty much free. Grace only had one gymnastics camp, but she and Meredith were going to stay in the States for *three whole weeks*, and I couldn't wait to have Bizzy all to myself.

Two weeks before the end of the semester, however, Bizzy told me that she had some wonderful news. She even had a smile on her face, but I knew instantly that something was wrong.

"What?" I asked.

"I'm being adopted."

"What?"

"Yes," she nodded. "I finally get to have a family."

I stared at her, unable to say anything.

"This is a good thing, Marco," she said when I still didn't speak.

"Where do they live?" I finally managed to ask. It could be somewhere close by . . . right here in Mexico City. That didn't happen very often, but it *did* happen . . .

"Canada."

"Canada?"

She nodded.

"You can't move to Canada!" I exclaimed.

"This is a good thing," she repeated.

"How is this a good thing?" I asked. "How can this possibly be a good thing?"

"I'm going to have a family, Marco," she said quietly. "I'm going to have a room of my own and a house with a yard and I'm going to get a Seeing Eye dog and go to college . . ."

I stared at her, dumbfounded.

"And I get to take real music lessons," she finished softly.

"We'll figure out a way for you to take music lessons here," I protested.

"This is a once-in-a-lifetime opportunity."

"But I'll never get to see you . . ."

"I know it's hard Marco, but—"

"What do you even know about these people?" I interrupted. I was distraught by the thought that she was going to move away, but I was also suspicious . . .

Who wants to adopt a fourteen-year-old kid?

"They're an older couple," she said. Then, as if reading my mind, she went on. "They've never been able to have kids of their own and they really want one, but they realize that it might not be very fair to adopt a baby since they're so much older . . ."

I shook my head in disgust and looked away, but then I started thinking.

What if Bizzy told them she didn't want to go with them? If Bizzy resisted the adoption hard enough, it probably wouldn't happen . . .

But how was I going to get her to do that?

Bizzy had the opportunity to have parents and a house and a yard and a dog and college and music lessons. A boyfriend with scars and nubs couldn't really compete with all that – especially since Bizzy wasn't going to have any problem getting another boyfriend if she wanted one.

No. There was no way I was going to be able to keep her here. Unless . . .

That evening I went into my dad's office. He glanced up at me from his computer.

"What's up?" he asked.

I didn't say anything but sat down on the couch that was along one wall. That couch had always been the go-to spot for us kids whenever we needed to talk with him, and he immediately got up from his computer and came to sit down next to me.

"What's up?" he asked again.

"Can we adopt Bizzy?"

"What?"

"Can we adopt Bizzy?" I repeated.

"Why?"

"So she can have a family," I explained. "She wants to have a mom and a dad and a house and pets and music lessons, and we can give her all that!"

I looked at him and realized he was actually considering it.

"Bizzy's already being adopted," Mom said, sticking her head in the door just long enough to ruin everything.

"But *we* could adopt her instead!" I exclaimed.

"Her new parents are very excited–" Mom began.

"They can get someone else," I said quickly.

"Why don't you want them to adopt her?" Dad asked.

"They live in Canada," Mom explained, casting a knowing glance at him over my head.

"Oh," Dad said dryly, and I knew I'd lost him.

"Please," I begged, looking back and forth between them. *"Please?!"*

"Marco," Mom began, looking at me patiently. "We can't–"

"Please?!" I interrupted, turning desperately to Dad.

He gave me a long look before he finally answered.

"Marco, you're not *dating* your sister."

I tried very hard not to cry the day Bizzy left, partly because (even though she couldn't *see* my tears) she might have heard them in my voice or felt them on my cheeks, and partly because I didn't want her new parents to see me cry. I also tried very hard not to hate them.

I didn't do a very good job on either count.

~ ~ ~

BIZZY AND I talked to each other almost every day at first after she left, but gradually that changed. Both of us started high school in the fall and our lives began revolving around homework and extracurricular activities. I tried not to take it personally if she didn't answer when I called or if she didn't return a message right away . . . both of us were very busy. Sometimes, however, it felt like she was a lot busier than I was.

There were always a lot of pictures of her online for me to look at. Often they were posted by her parents: pictures of her in their boat on Lake Ontario . . . of her performing in concerts with her new violin . . . of her posing with her new Seeing Eye dog (a black lab named Star).

But a lot of them were posted by her new friends, too: pictures of her and a group of girls with their faces covered in paint at a professional hockey game . . . pictures of her and some friends playing with little kids at some kind of church picnic . . . pictures of her and her classmates on the observation deck of the CN Tower in Toronto.

The one that worried me had been taken at lunch in their school cafeteria. It was of a group of kids – about eight total – and Bizzy was on the perimeter. Next to her was some guy with his arm draped over her shoulder . . . some guy with no visible scars . . . some guy with ten good-looking fingers.

I studied that picture endlessly and obsessed over it, searching for any clues I could find as to who he was and what he meant to her. Maybe he was the friendly sort who put his arm around every girl he knew. Maybe he was just reining her in to make sure she would fit in the frame.

Or maybe Bizzy had moved on.

I agonized over this thought and I worried about it constantly . . .

But I never did manage to work up the nerve to ask.

~ ~ ~

MEANWHILE, HOWEVER, LIFE went on.

Puberty finally hit hard enough that I appropriated a razor from Grace's drawer in the bathroom and started shaving every day. The scientific part of my brain told me that there was no possible way that what you did to the *dead* hair on the outside of your skin could affect the *living* hair on the inside of your skin, but I had heard enough people say that shaving would make your hair come in thicker and fuller, so I didn't figure it was going to hurt anything to try.

"I know you took it," Grace accused one day when I denied having any idea where her razor was.

"I did not."

"You're a terrible liar," she said, "and you're so stupid too. You don't even have any stupid hair growing on your ugly, stupid lip."

"That's because I shaved it off!"

"Yeah – with *my* razor."

She went off to whine about it to Mom and I made a special point not to care. I definitely had hair growing above my lip, no matter what Grace said.

Every day I ran my hand across my upper lip, noting what was going on and trying to coax the follicles to cooperate. I would stop shaving for a few days to see what the progress was and then start again in hopes of encouraging all that thicker, fuller growth I'd heard so much about.

After two months, however, I finally looked into the mirror one day and had to admit the truth.

"Something's wrong."

I had waited to say that until after I'd stepped into my dad's office and closed the door, keeping my voice low in case Grace was lurking in the hall.

"What's wrong?" he asked, turning away from his computer.

I sat down on the couch and he came over and sat down next to me.

"My moustache isn't growing right," I told him.

"You have a moustache?" he asked. I think he was trying very, very hard not to laugh.

"Look," I said, grabbing his hand and bringing it to my face. "It's growing here," I rubbed one of his fingers above the corner of my lip on one side, "and here," I rubbed it on the other side, "but not *here*." That time I put his finger on the spot right above my lip, directly under my nose.

He looked at me for a moment, apparently no longer about to laugh, and then he spoke carefully.

"Marco," he said softly. "I don't think it's *going* to grow there."

"Why not?"

"It's scar tissue," he explained. "Hair doesn't grow on scar tissue."

He lifted the hem of his shorts to show me a scar on his thigh that he'd gotten when he fell out of a tree about fifteen years earlier. It was shiny and smooth, tight and hairless.

"I'm not going to be able to grow a moustache?" I asked, mortified. I was so upset that I forgot to keep my voice down.

"I don't think so," he said sympathetically, shaking his head.

"How come you never told me?"

"I . . . I guess I never thought about it," he admitted.

"You never thought about it?" I cried. It was *all* I'd been thinking about. "I was going to grow a moustache to hide my scar!"

"You can't even see your scar–" he began, but I cut him off.

"Yes, you can!" I yelled. "*I* can!"

"Look, Marco," he said. "I understand–"

"No, you don't," I shouted, interrupting him again. "You don't understand! You don't understand anything at all!"

And I stormed out of his office, slamming the door behind me.

Two days later, Dad called me into his office. He was sitting on the couch with his laptop and I slouched in and started to sit down, but he stopped me and told me to close the door.

I obeyed before reluctantly joining him on the couch.

He made sure I was looking at him before turning the screen in my direction.

"Look at this," he said.

I gave the monitor a cursory glance, but when I realized what I was looking at, I leaned forward, studying it harder, barely able to believe what I was seeing.

Leading plastic surgeon . . . facial hair transplants . . . moustache region . . . designed to restore hair . . . conceals scarring . . . donor hairs obtained from the scalp . . . grows like normal facial hair . . . can be shaved . . . permanent . . . precision placement of the grafts at exact angles assure naturalness . . . microscopically dissected grafts minimize scarring . . .

When I finally dared to look away from the computer, Dad was staring at me intently. I didn't say one word.

"Do you want this?" he asked quietly.

I gaped at him.

"Are you serious?" I managed in a voice just above a whisper.

He nodded and I continued to stare at him. I could barely breathe.

"Do you want to get it done?" he asked.

"Yes."

He nodded again.

"Did you talk to Mom about it?" I asked, because this was just too good to be true.

He nodded for a third time and said, "She's completely against it."

I looked at him questioningly.

"But she'll get over it," he said.

I narrowed my eyes doubtfully.

"Don't worry about your mother," he assured me quietly. "This is something only a man would understand." And he gave me a small, conspiratorial smile.

"When?" I asked.

"Three weeks."

"Three weeks?"

"I went ahead and made an appointment. We have to fly to Boston . . . I'll buy the tickets this afternoon."

"Boston?"

He pointed to the screen. "This guy's one of the best in the world. If we're going to do this, we're going to do it right."

I resisted the urge to hug him, nodding instead and looking at the computer again, trying to wrap my brain around how everything in my life had just changed in the past two minutes.

"But Marco?" Dad said, interrupting my thoughts.

I looked back to him.

"What?"

"I want to tell you something."

I should have known there would be a catch.

"What?"

He rested his eyes on me and paused for a long moment before he spoke.

"The only reason I'm doing this," he said, reaching out and touching my arm, "is because I know how important it is to you."

He paused.

"I don't want you to think for one single second," he went on, "that I'm doing this because I think that there's anything wrong with you."

I didn't say anything.

"Do you understand what I'm saying?"

I managed to nod at him.

"I don't think you *need* to have this done," he explained further. "I'm only doing it because I know that you *want* to have it done."

I couldn't answer.

"The very first day I laid eyes on you," he said, looking away as if he were remembering, "I thought that you were absolutely perfect."

He brought his eyes back to me and held my gaze intently.

"I still think that," he finished. "I want to make sure you know that."

I finally managed to find my voice. "I know," I said.

This time I didn't resist the urge to hug him.

Three weeks later, I missed a whole week of school – another thing Mom had a fit about. It was a quiet fit, however, because Dad had insisted that nobody else needed to know any details about what kind of surgery I was going to have and Mom didn't have many chances to voice her opinions when Grace or Meredith weren't around. When I was little, I'd had several surgeries because of my cleft, and Dad didn't have any problem telling my sisters that we were simply going to "fix some things that still weren't quite right." Grace looked briefly suspicious, but Dad was a much better liar than I was, so thankfully she let it rest.

Three weeks later we flew to Boston on a Monday and had our consultation on Tuesday. Wednesday I had my surgery. It lasted almost four hours and I was awake the whole time, but I didn't feel a thing and felt so good afterward that we went to Mike's Pastry and split a lobster tail (which, it turns out, is not really lobster at all). Thursday I had a follow-up appointment that lasted all of about three minutes, and that night we went to see the Red Sox play the Cubs. Friday we flew home.

For two weeks I kept a dressing over my upper lip and Grace out of my business. The stitches dissolved and the transplanted hairs fell out the way I'd been told they would, and when they started growing back right on schedule two months later the way they were supposed to, Dad bought me an electric razor.

I threw Grace's stupid disposable one in the trash.

Once my moustache finally came in and covered my scar almost completely, I was close to being able to convince myself that I looked normal.

One day, when I was home alone, I stood in front of the mirror in Mom and Dad's bathroom and put my hands behind my back. I stared at my reflection.

After a moment, I went into Dad's office and took his favorite leather jacket from the hook on the back of his door. I put it on and went back to their bathroom. I stuffed my hands into the pockets of the jacket, and I looked into the mirror again.

This time, I almost liked what I saw.

BIZZY AND I continued to keep in touch throughout high school. She knew everything that had happened in my life since she'd left, just like I knew everything that had happened in hers. She knew that my grandmother had died the summer after my freshman year. She knew that I'd had an assist on the winning goal of our championship soccer game during my sophomore year. She knew that I'd gotten to go to Los Angeles as a senior when I'd won a design challenge hosted by Tec Santa Fe. She knew about my moustache.

Likewise, I knew that her parents had taken her on a cruise to Alaska for her sixteenth birthday. I knew that she'd been chosen as a finalist in an international violin competition and had flown to Germany during her junior year to perform with the Berlin Philharmonic Orchestra. I knew that she'd served as a camp counselor at a Christian camp in the Kawartha Highlands for the past two summers. I knew that her father was going to retire as soon as Bizzy was through with school.

What I didn't know, however, was whether or not Bizzy was still my girlfriend. We hadn't exactly broken up or anything, but we also hadn't seen each other in four years. And while we still wrapped up our conversations with our usual "I love you's," they seemed a lot less romantic and a lot more friendly-like than they once had.

There had been more pictures over the years of her with more guys, too. Guys who had nothing wrong with them. Guys who might have been just friends . . . or who might have been more.

In four years, I had still never worked up the nerve to ask.

By the time I graduated from high school, I may not have known where things stood between me and Bizzy, but at least I knew what I wanted to do with my life. My dad (an engineer) had been steering me toward his profession ever since I was little. It really wasn't too hard of a sell because I loved everything about math and science, and engineering was the perfect combination of the two. The only thing I was unsure of was what *type* of engineer I wanted to be, but Dad – unintentionally – had helped me figure that out too.

Just as he'd always tried to figure out ways to minimize the impact of my cleft palate, Dad had also studied every potential treatment for symbrachydactyly that he could find. There are definitely some things that can be done if you have symbrachydactyly, but unfortunately, each treatment comes with its own set of problems.

One thing doctors can do for you is to take bones from your toes and graft them onto your hands. They do this usually when you're really little – like two. Then, when you're older, you can go through a process called "distraction lengthening." It involves a number of surgeries and a device called a distractor, which has two metal pins that are inserted through the upper and lower portions of your finger bones and are connected by rods. They cut the bone between the pins and rods and use the distractor to create a gap, which will get filled in with new bone tissue and make the fingers longer.

Mom and Dad had been required to make a decision about that process long before I even understood that anything was wrong with me. I was already going through a lot of surgeries at that time because of my cleft, and the results of toe grafting didn't seem super promising. Any new fingers formed are a lot smaller than normal ones and they often aren't aligned with the hands properly. Movement is usually limited, too, plus it was likely that I would have had trouble running or walking if toe bones were removed.

Ultimately, Mom and Dad had decided against it.

Another option if you have symbrachydactyly is to have only your second toe removed and transferred onto your hand.

They do this a lot if someone already has a thumb, like I do, because it gives the thumb something to pinch against (and just having your second toe removed doesn't usually cause problems with running and walking the way having the bones of lots of toes removed does). This is something that can be done when you're older, so Mom and Dad decided that I could choose that later for myself if I wanted to.

I decided against it.

Mom and Dad had never let me use my hands as an excuse for anything and had always acted as if I could do everything that everybody else could . . . and so I could. Sure, I might need to use a pencil or my teeth to help me do something, but I learned how to button and zip and tie and how to write and to type. I could scrub and scrape and clean, cut and chop and peel. Mom made sure I could do dishes, and Dad made sure I could throw and catch. There was really nothing that I couldn't do. (Except play the violin. Bizzy had tried to teach me once, and I was horrible at it. Honestly though, I don't think that really had anything to do with my hands.) And so, when I got older, I decided that I didn't really want to have a toe transplanted onto my hand – I just didn't figure it was worth it.

Prosthetics are another option if you have symbrachydactyly. There are several types.

One is cosmetic prosthetics. These are very lifelike (complete with hair and freckles) and their main purpose is to help you look normal. I had a set once but found I could hardly do anything when I had them on. They seemed to slow down every movement I made and felt so unnatural that I wound up stuffing them into the back of a drawer, resigning myself to the fact that I was forever going to look like a freak.

Another type of prosthetics you can get, however, is called neural prosthetics . . . and neural prosthetics changed my life (but not in the way you might be thinking).

Although there are lots of different types of neural prosthetics, essentially they all have one thing in common: they work with your nervous system to help make up for whatever it is that you're missing.

My sister Lily has a really common type of neural prosthetic. She was born deaf, and when she was little, she got cochlear implants. Doctors attached a series of tiny electrodes to her auditory nerves, and then to receivers. Small microphones, processors, and transmitters attach to the outside of her head by magnets, and the sounds picked up by the microphone are passed from the processor to the transmitter to the receiver and at last to the electrodes. The electrodes stimulate her auditory nerve so that Lily can hear. There are neural prosthetic devices for just about everything you can imagine: arms, legs, hands . . . even fingers.

About a year after I got my moustache, Dad took me to Philadelphia to investigate neural prosthetics. The type we were looking at were very advanced, with sensors that picked up on subtle chemical and electrical currents from the muscles in my hands to control the prosthetic fingers. There was a definite learning curve, but by the end of one week I was able to use the prosthetic fingers to spear a piece of steak with my fork and cut it with my knife. I could also pick up a blueberry without crushing it and wind thread onto a bobbin (which, incidentally, was not something I planned on doing a whole lot of).

Ultimately, however, we decided against getting neural prosthetics. They seemed to slow me down almost as much as the cosmetic prosthetics had because I had to think so hard to make them do whatever I wanted them to do. Supposedly everything would have become second nature to me after a while, but I didn't see much point in getting them since I could already do everything that I wanted anyway. I was so used to my hands the way they were that I worried these new prosthetics would wind up in the back of a drawer like the other set had . . . and these were *way* too expensive to let that happen.

So I ultimately left Philadelphia without any prosthetics, but I also left with a certainty of what I wanted to do with my life. I might have decided against neural prosthetics for myself, but the technology behind them was cutting-edge and amazing, and I knew that I wanted to be a part of it.

I started looking into universities around the world and – when the time came – concentrated on the ones that were leading the way in biomedical engineering. In December of my senior year, my top choice, Princeton, accepted me, and Mom and Dad took me out to eat to celebrate. Then, two weeks later – when Grace made the decision to attend school in California (on the other side of the continent) – I celebrated again.

~ ~ ~

EARLY ON DURING my first semester at Princeton, I took an anatomy and physiology course. During one of our labs, while I was busy hooking electrodes up to the sciatic nerve of a pithed frog (to collect data about the relationship between stimulus intensity and response), our professor wrapped up her verbal instructions.

"After you've made sure that the stimulus amplitude is at zero point two five volts and the pulse width is at zero point one, you should go ahead and apply a brief stimulus at the proximal end of the nerve."

I was ready to go so I hit the button and then read the computer screen. She walked by as I was recording the numbers, and I looked up at her.

"Is this basically how they figure out where to place an electrode array in a cochlear implant?" I asked.

"Well," she shrugged, "it's a lot more sophisticated, obviously, but yeah. Basically it's the same principle."

I nodded.

"How do you know about cochlear implants?" she wanted to know.

"My sister has them," I explained, and she nodded understandingly.

"Can you imagine trying to get about a thousand of those placed just right?" she asked with a laugh.

"A thousand?" I knew that Lily's array only had about thirty electrodes in it and I didn't think things had advanced *that* much since she'd gotten hers. Plus, I was also was pretty sure that limb prosthetics didn't have that many either.

"Optic nerves," she said knowingly. "Major precision."
"Oh."

"Of course it's still in its infancy compared to what they're doing with cochlears," she shrugged, "but you know . . . it's just a matter of time."

"Yeah," I agreed.

After lab that day, I researched everything I could find about visual prostheses: the tiny cameras and transmitters, the neural interfaces of electrode array cuffs, the surgery to access the optic nerve . . .

It would likely be years before the technology even came close to approaching that of other neural prosthetics, but I couldn't wait to call Bizzy anyway.

"Guess what I've been looking into?" I asked her.

"What?"

"Visual prosthetics!"

"You mean like bionic eyes?"

"You already know about them?" I asked, slightly disheartened.

"Well, yeah," she said. "But it's not like it's going to help me anytime soon."

"No," I admitted, "but I've been studying up on it and it's pretty cool."

"I suppose," she said.

"I think that's what I want to do."

"What do you mean?" she asked.

"I mean I think that's what I want to go into," I replied. "Visual prosthetics."

"Are you serious?"

If there was another field in the area of biomedical engineering that was as advanced as this one, I didn't know about it. Plus, Bizzy sounded pretty pleased.

"Yeah," I said. "I think so."

We talked for a bit longer and then she said that she needed to study.

"I miss you, Bizzy."

"I miss you, too," she said.

It was almost a singsong voice . . . the same one she used to tell me that she loved me, too. It was the voice that made me feel like she didn't really miss me at all.

"No, Bizzy," I said. "I mean I really, really miss you."

There was a slight hesitation, but then she said, in a much softer voice, "I really miss you, too."

"I was thinking that maybe I'd drive up there and see you sometime."

"To Montreal?"

"It's only about seven hours."

There was another hesitation.

"If you don't want me to–" I began, but she cut me off.

"No," she said. "That would be great if you're sure that's what you want to do."

"I'm sure."

"Okay," she agreed. "When?"

I went over my fall break.

I couldn't eat the day I left, and the closer I got to Montreal the more nervous I became. By the time I checked into my hotel and dropped my stuff off, I was on the verge of throwing up – even though my stomach was completely empty.

I drove to the parking deck that Bizzy had told me to go to and texted her to let her know that I had arrived, counting on her text-to-voice translator to sound a lot more calm and collected than my own voice would have. She texted me back and told me to meet her by the main entrance of the parking deck. She said she'd be there in five minutes.

Those five minutes seemed almost as long as the entire drive to Montreal had. Finally, however, I spotted her coming down the sidewalk toward me, holding tight to her dog Star's lead. I headed in her direction, wiping my sweaty palms on my pants.

"Bizzy," I managed to say as I neared her.

"Hace tiempo que no te veo . . ."

Long time, no see, Marco.

She broke into a broad smile and opened her arms for a hug.

Bizzy introduced me to Star and then asked me if I was hungry. I told her that I was (even though I still wasn't really sure I was going to be able to keep anything down) and by the time we got to the restaurant, I found that I was really glad she had a dog. Not only was I happy that Bizzy had the pet she'd always wanted and that Star allowed her a whole new level of freedom compared to what she'd known before, but I was also thankful to Star for helping me avoid all those awkward moments of silence that I knew would have hung in the air otherwise. Just having Star wag her tail at me when I first reached down to pet her put me somewhat at ease, and as the evening went on I found that any time an uncomfortable lull in the conversation arose, I could just ask Bizzy a question about Star and we'd suddenly have something else to talk about. That plan got me through the end of dinner (by which time I knew more about Seeing Eye dogs than most other people in North America combined).

"So I gather it would be bad if I fed her a French fry?" I asked as Bizzy finished off the last of her drink.

"Very bad," Bizzy laughed.

"Sorry, Star," I said, looking down at the dog. "I tried."

Bizzy laughed again.

I looked at her for a moment as she put down her glass, trying to read her face . . . trying for the millionth time to figure out exactly where I stood with her.

Just the fact that she'd agreed to let me come up here to see her said something, didn't it? Didn't she *have* to know that I wouldn't have driven all this way to see her if all I viewed her as was just a friend? Surely she must have known that there was more to it than that.

"You're awfully quiet," Bizzy noted. "Everything okay?"

"Yeah," I said. "I was just wondering if you're ready to go."

"Sure," she said. "What do you want to do now?"

"Um, maybe we could take a walk," I suggested.

"Sure," she said again. "Let's go."

Bizzy always kept Star on her left side, so I made sure that I set out on her right. We walked along in silence for a few moments because I couldn't think up anything else to ask her about her dog.

"You're awfully quiet," she commented again.

"Just thinking what a shame it is that you don't need me anymore." I said it lightheartedly, with a deliberate laugh in my voice.

"What do you mean?"

"You used to hold my arm all the time," I said. "But now that you've got Star you don't need to."

"I didn't *need* to then," she smiled. "I just did it because I wanted to."

"Oh," I said, and she slipped her arm through mine.

After we'd walked for a few minutes, we came to a bench, and – emboldened by the fact that she was still holding my arm – I suggested that we sit down together. She agreed.

We sat in silence and it didn't seem so awkward anymore. She didn't ask me why I was so quiet and I didn't ask her about her dog. After a moment, I got up the nerve to reach my free hand out and touch her cheek, catching a stray piece of her dark, wavy hair with my thumb and gently brushing it from her face.

She turned toward me and I looked at her for a long moment.

"I've missed you," I finally told her.

"I've missed you, too," she answered softly.

"I've missed *us*," I clarified.

"Me, too."

"Really?"

"Yes," she nodded. "Why do you sound so surprised?"

I pressed my lips together and sighed quietly.

"Because sometimes I wonder if there even is an 'us', Bizzy."

"What do you mean?" she asked, looking confused.

"I mean I don't know what's going on between you and me."

"What do you mean?" she asked again.

"I mean I want to know where I stand with you," I said. "I want to know what I am to you."

"You're my boyfriend," she answered carefully.

"I am?"

"Well I *thought* you were," she said, "but if that's not what you want–"

"No," I said hastily, "it *is* what I want, but I just wasn't sure because . . ."

"Because what?" she asked when I hesitated.

"Because I just wasn't sure," I said softly.

She didn't say anything.

"I love you," I told her quietly.

"I love you, too."

"No," I said. "I mean I really, *really* love you."

"I really love you, too," she replied, a smile beginning to form on her lips.

I reached out and touched the side of her face and I watched that smile that I loved so much spread and reach up to her eyes. Then I leaned forward and pressed my lips against hers and Star nudged my hand with her cold, wet nose. I rubbed the top of her head to let her know that everything was all right, and I kept on kissing Bizzy as if I hadn't kissed her in over four years.

I drove to Canada a lot during college – either to Montreal to visit her while she was at school or to Ontario, where her parents lived in Peterborough. Her mom and dad were always very nice to me, and I didn't hate them anymore for taking Bizzy away from me when I was fourteen. They took me to a bakery in Bobcaygeon where I had some kind of pastry called a Chelsea bun that tasted even better than the lobster tail I'd had in Boston with my dad, and then they took me to the lift lock on the Trent-Severn Waterway, where they seemed very amused by my fascination with it.

"You know we have a boat, right?" her father asked. "We can go on it if you want." And the next thing I knew, I was on the Trent-Severn Waterway, riding on my first lift lock.

In the winter, Bizzy and I went skating on the canal, and her parents brought her to Princeton several times since she was considering going to graduate school at Curtis Institute of Music in Philadelphia, which wasn't too far away. When they visited me, we went to orchards and wineries, and one day I took them to Mercer Lake, hoping that we'd get to catch some rowing.

As it turned out, we did more than just "catch some rowing." An instructor was just finishing up an introductory class as we arrived and she stopped to pet Star (something that happened a lot when we were out). We talked with the instructor for a little while and – before we knew it – we were in a boat, having a free, impromptu lesson. Star sat in front of the instructor, calmly keeping her eye on things as the four of us tried our hands at sculling and Bizzy was amazed by all of it (but mostly by the fact that she had never before realized that when you're rowing, you're facing backward).

By the time I started my senior year, I was ready to ask Bizzy to marry me. I figured we'd be engaged for our last year at school and then get married in the summer before graduate school started.

Bizzy wasn't cooperating a whole lot with my plans, however. I was still planning on entering the field of retinal neuroprosthetics and had decided to go to Australia to study at the University of Melbourne. They were teamed with a major vision prosthetics group that was leading the way in research and clinical trials, and I really wanted to be a part of it all. I'd been hinting around to Bizzy for a long time that she needed to consider going to graduate school in Australia too, but she didn't seem to be taking any of my suggestions too seriously. Once I got officially accepted into their graduate program, however, I did more than drop little hints. I flat-out asked her why she hadn't applied.

"I can't go with you to Australia," she said, sounding surprised that I didn't already know this.

"Why not?"

"Because I'm going to go to Curtis."

"Why are you moving fifty minutes away from Princeton *now*?" I cried. "Why didn't you transfer three years ago?"

"Because I've always wanted to get my bachelor's degree from Montreal and I want to go to graduate school at Curtis."

"Haven't you ever wanted to be near me?"

"Well of course I have," she said gently, "and I *do*. But right now this is something that I need to do."

"But Melbourne's got a great graduate program in music," I argued.

"Is it the one I've been dreaming of going to since I was fifteen?" she asked.

"Well, no, but–"

"Marco," she interrupted quietly. "I'm not going to Australia."

I looked at her for a long moment.

"But we're going to be so far apart," I said unhappily.

"We've been apart for a long time," she reminded me, "and we've been doing fine."

"I don't like being apart."

"We'll be fine."

I also hinted around that we should get engaged, but Bizzy never jumped on the idea the way I needed her to, and just like I was too insecure in high school to ask her where things stood between the two of us, I was too scared now to find out whether or not she wanted to be my wife.

~ ~ ~

IN AUSTRALIA, EVERYTHING is upside down. The water swirls clockwise when it goes down drains, Christmas is in the summer, and everybody drives on the wrong side of the road. Another thing that's different is that universities start their school year in February and end in October. Fortunately, however, the program I was entering allowed me to start at the beginning of their second semester in late July – after I graduated from Princeton in May.

Dad did some research on housing and decided that he wanted to purchase a place for me to live while I was in Melbourne, insisting that it would be a good investment as long as I got a roommate to help cover the bills. Before I left, I advertised for a roommate (which, incidentally, I learned is actually called a *flatmate*) and found someone who was interested – a guy named Peter who was halfway through his master's degree in urban horticulture. He said that he played cricket and the guitar and enjoyed surfing, and I told him I'd see him in July.

I arrived in Australia and moved what few things I'd brought with me into the modest house that Dad had found. It had two little bedrooms with a small bath between them, a tiny front yard and an even tinier backyard. I bought a little table and two chairs for the kitchen, a bed, a dresser, nightstand, and lamp for my bedroom, and a futon, coffee table, and television for the living room. Then I splurged on two nice wrought-iron patio chairs for the front porch. (I noticed that the sun set right in front of the house, and I decided that I wanted to be able to sit and watch it.)

I went to a thrift store and purchased some pots, pans, dishes, silverware, a coffeemaker, and a toaster for the kitchen. I didn't really plan on using the kitchen much, but I had promised Peter that everything would be furnished except for what he wanted for his bedroom, and I kind of felt that the cupboards shouldn't be bare. Last I bought a small used car that promised excellent gas mileage and a decent resale value. Then I went and checked out the university.

Princeton had been small and quaint, but Melbourne was huge and almost overwhelming. I liked it a lot though, and I couldn't wait to get started in my program. I introduced myself to my academic advisor and was taken on a tour of the research facility. After that I filled out some paperwork, got a parking pass, and had lunch at a crowded café on campus. Finally, I got back in my car and headed for St. Kilda.

I'd read about St. Kilda before moving and had made up my mind that I was going to check it out as soon as I could.

I wound up liking it as much as I liked the university.

There were shops and rides, and it was crowded and funky and eclectic, and the beach was beautiful, with gentle waves that lapped softly at the shore. I went for a walk along one of the paths and then settled onto the sandy beach for a while to take everything in.

All around me were people walking, talking, laughing. Two young men played Frisbee and I watched them for a long time, beginning to feel lonelier and lonelier as time went on. I wished my brother or my dad were here with me, and I started to really look forward to Peter arriving the next day, hoping that the two of us were going to get along well so that I would have someone to do something with.

Then a young couple walked past me, holding hands.

I missed Bizzy.

On the way home from the beach, I saw an advertisement for an animal sanctuary, so the next morning, I decided to go pay it a visit. Peter had told me he wasn't going to move in until late afternoon, and I was hoping I would get to see a koala or a platypus or something. As it turned out, the sanctuary was really just a retirement home for kangaroos who couldn't make it in the wild, but I'd never seen a kangaroo before either, so I made a donation at the door, grabbed an informational brochure, and went on in.

The sanctuary had several areas, but the main attraction was a huge, fenced-in enclosure with a large, grassy yard. I entered cautiously to find myself in the company of dozens of kangaroos, and I put some money in a little food dispenser to get a handful of pellets before I took a look around.

There were a few kangaroos ambling across the grass, but most of them were dozing lazily in the sun. I knelt beside a sleeping animal who was not even interested enough in me or my food to bother lifting its head. I reached out to pet it, gently scratching behind its ears.

As I did, I thought about how much Bizzy loved animals, and I imagined that her face would light up with that smile of hers if she was with me now. Ever since I fell in love with Bizzy over eight years earlier, I had always tried to see things through her eyes (or lack thereof). Every time I did something new, I found myself imagining how Bizzy might experience it . . . how it would feel to her, or sound, or smell.

So now, as I ran my hands down the kangaroo's body and stroked its soft fur, I closed my eyes and imagined how it would feel to Bizzy. I rubbed its belly and – as I did – I realized that I was petting a female. I could tell because I could feel the opening to her pouch.

I opened my eyes to look at her and then I dumped my handful of food onto the grass in front of her nose. She stretched her head out far enough to take a sniff, but then she went back to ignoring it. Meanwhile, I rubbed her belly with both hands. I was no kangaroo expert, but after a minute I was pretty sure she didn't have a joey.

What did the inside of a kangaroo's pouch feel like?
Could I actually stick my hand in there and find out?
I glanced around.
Would that be a weird thing to do?
Would she would kick me unconscious if I did?
Finally I decided that it really shouldn't be much different than rubbing a dog's belly, and I made up my mind to go for it. I glanced around one more time to make sure no one was watching, and then I closed my eyes again, tentatively slid my hand into her pouch, and hoped for the best.

The kangaroo acted even less interested with the fact that I had my hand inside her pouch than she did with the pile of food I'd put in front of her nose. It wasn't furry inside like I'd expected, but it was very warm and soft – like a flannel blanket.

I knew for sure that if Bizzy was with me, she would definitely be smiling.

That afternoon I received a text from Peter telling me that he had lost his scholarship and wasn't going to be rooming with me after all.

Sorry, mate.

Sorry, mate?

I called my dad and broke the news to him. He sighed.

"Try to find another roommate," he said.

"Flatmate, Dad," I corrected him. "They're called flatmates."

"I don't care what they're called," he said. "Just try to find one."

"I'm not going to be able to find anyone now," I protested. "It's the middle of the school year here – I was lucky to find Peter in the first place! Everybody's already got a place to live."

"Just try," he insisted. "If you can't find someone then I'll cover it, but you've got to at least try."

"I'll try," I promised, but I had a feeling it was going to be a complete and total waste of time.

Because I had promised, I placed an ad with a couple of "flatmate finder" services, and then I went to the student union and learned that I could advertise on one of several notice boards available, as long as I had the ad approved before I posted it. I printed up a small ad and showed it to the work-study student on duty so that she could approve it. She looked it over, stamped it, and then handed it back for me to post on a board.

"You should also advertise online," she suggested as I took it from her. *That's* when she noticed my hands.

"I did," I said. "Thanks."

I ignored the look on her face – a cross between shock and revulsion – and I headed off toward the nearest notice board.

Once there I perused the board, looking for a good spot, and I discovered that there were no other advertisements for roommates (and none for flatmates either). This was probably because everybody already *had* a place to live (just like I'd already told Dad), but I posted my ad anyhow and headed away.

I had only made it about twenty feet or so before someone rushed up behind me.

"Excuse me?"

I turned to find a woman about my age with an anxious look on her face.

"I, um, I'm sorry," she said, holding up in front of me the very ad that I had just posted. "I know it says you're looking for a *male* housemate, but . . ."

I looked at her in surprise.

"My name's Josette," she said hastily, sticking out her hand.

I put my hand in hers and shook it . . .

She didn't even flinch.

"I really need a place to stay," she went on, indicating my ad again. "I know it says 'Male', but since it's two bedrooms I thought that maybe . . ."

Her voice trailed off as she looked at me helplessly.

"You'll hardly even know I'm there," she finished quietly. "I *really* need a place to stay."

I studied her for a moment. She didn't just look anxious, she looked . . . desperate. There was something about her . . .

Something sad.

Something needful.

I thought for a moment.

Mom and Dad had spent their whole lives teaching me that we're supposed to do whatever we can to help other people . . . and this girl really seemed to need help. Plus, Dad hadn't specified exactly what *kind* of a roommate to get, had he? And he didn't want to pay the whole mortgage by himself, did he?

"Sure," I finally shrugged. "Why not?"

I had really liked how she hadn't even flinched when she'd touched my hand.

~ ~ ~

JOSETTE HADN'T BEEN kidding when she'd said that I would hardly even know she was there – she was like the Invisible Roommate.

I had given her a key the day we met, and when I came home from the university the next day she was apparently all moved in. After that, it seemed that she was gone all day, every day – even on Sundays – but it was hard to tell for sure because she kept her door closed whether she was there or not. When she *was* home, she only came out long enough to dart into the bathroom from time to time, shutting her bedroom door tightly behind her whenever she did.

Occasionally she would arrive home from wherever she spent her days while I was in the living room or the kitchen, but she would invariably give me a brief wave and a nod, muttering something that sounded like "Hello" before ducking quickly into her bedroom for the rest of the evening.

I never saw her using the kitchen, although sometimes I would come home and catch a faint, telltale whiff of something having been cooked while I was gone. Aside from a few ramen noodle wrappers in the trash, however, she left no evidence that she had ever even been there.

Although I was pretty lonely and wouldn't have minded having some company in the evenings or on the weekends, having Josette for a roommate wasn't so bad. I found that I never had to clean the bathroom (it always seemed spotless) and the few times I left a dirty bowl or plate in the sink, it would get mysteriously washed, dried, and put away while I was at school. Things could definitely have been worse.

I loved my classes and my research. Most of the guys I did research with were married and had lives of their own, but everyone was pretty nice, and the sophistication of what we were working on was like a dream come true. Compared to cochlear implants and other prosthetic devices, there was still a long way to go, but I was right there on the cutting edge – one of the ones who was making it happen.

I couldn't have been happier.

Well, that's not true. I could have had a roommate who liked to play Frisbee or cards or something like that. I could have had friends at school who wanted to go out to dinner or who wanted to see a movie from time to time. I could have had a girlfriend who was going to graduate school with me in Australia.

So, yeah . . . I could have been happier, but overall, things were pretty good.

Not long after Josette moved in, I pulled out of my driveway and drove to the end of the block, where I found her standing on the corner. I pulled up beside her and rolled down my window.

"You need a ride?" I asked.

She seemed startled to see me.

"Oh, no," she said, shaking her head. "I'm just waiting for the bus."

"I don't mind giving you a ride," I insisted. "Where are you going?"

"Work," she said hesitantly, "but I'll just take the bus."

"I don't mind," I said again.

She shook her head a second time.

"It's coming now," she explained, pointing down the street.

I looked in my rearview mirror, saw the bus, and got out of the way so that it could pick her up.

The public transportation system in Melbourne was quite good and a lot of people who lived there didn't even bother owning a car, but I still felt kind of funny whenever I saw Josette waiting for the bus because I could have easily given her a ride wherever she was going. After getting turned down a few more times, however, I quit asking. I just gave her a little wave whenever I passed by and went on my way.

I usually picked up some takeout food or cooked something simple for myself in the evenings, and I ate at the coffee table while I watched TV. Before long I was trying to sit down in front of the television around seven o'clock so that I could watch a game show I'd discovered called *Chances Are*.

The show was hosted by a man named Wally Fletcher and was played in a series of rounds. The first question they asked was always real easy: *What character wanted a heart in* The Wizard of Oz? (The Tin Man.)

Whoever buzzed in first and answered correctly then had the option of progressing further with more questions built upon the theme introduced with the first question.

What was the name of the original actor slated to play the Tin Man? (Buddy Ebsen.)

What substance caused him to relinquish his role due to an allergic reaction? (Aluminum dust.)

In what comedy series did Ebsen star from 1962 to 1971? (The Beverly Hillbillies.)

In what drama series did Ebsen play the title character from 1973 to 1980? (Barnaby Jones.)

And so on and so on, until the questions finally got so hard that they were pretty much unanswerable: *What was Ebsen's given name?* (Christian.)

I usually did pretty good – especially if the questions had anything to do with science or technology – and I started looking forward to watching it in the evenings. He wasn't as good as Bizzy or Dorito, but all things considered, Wally wasn't bad company.

~ ~ ~

NOT TOO LONG after Josette had moved in, I woke up in the middle of the night and got out of bed, heading for the bathroom. When I got to the hallway, however, I found that the bathroom door was closed and I realized that Josette was already in there.

Her bedroom door, next to the bathroom, was open. Not open much actually, just slightly . . . but enough that I could see into her room if I got close enough and really craned my neck (which I did).

The light was on and I saw two suitcases and three cardboard boxes. There was no furniture whatsoever, and several blankets, along with a pillow, were spread out on the floor.

The toilet flushed and the sound of it sent me tiptoeing quickly back to my room, closing the door quietly before the water in the sink had even started to run.

The next afternoon I knocked on Josette's bedroom door, unsure if she was even home or not.

"Yes?" she called.

"Can I talk to you for a minute?"

I stepped back from the door as she opened it slightly and peered at me through the crack.

"Yes?" she said again.

"Can you come out here?" I asked. I stepped back even farther, and she opened her door just wide enough to slip out into the hallway. She closed the door quickly behind her and looked at me expectantly.

"I went to the grocery store today," I began, "and they were having this huge special on ribeyes. There were two in a package and I thought I'd grill them up tonight and then take one of them to work to heat up for lunch tomorrow, but I just remembered that I have this thing to go to tomorrow and I don't want it to go to waste and I wondered if maybe you liked steak?"

I took a breath from my rambling, and she looked at me carefully.

"A thing?" she finally asked.

"Yeah." I nodded. "Some intern thing with sandwiches and stuff . . . and I think maybe shrimp."

Sandwiches and shrimp?

"So, anyway," I went on, "I'm not that great of a cook or anything, but I don't want it to go to waste and . . ."

"I don't want to take your food," she said, shaking her head. "You could just wait and cook the other one tomorrow night or something."

"Eh," I said, waving my hand at her. "I don't really want to mess with the grill two nights in a row. If you don't want it, I can just throw away what I don't eat. It's no big deal, they were really cheap."

"Don't throw it away," she said hastily. "I'll eat whatever you don't want."

"Great. You want a salad, too?"

"Well . . ."

"That stuff's just going to go to waste too . . ."

"I guess so," she said hesitantly. "If you're sure."

"Sure, I'm sure," I said, smiling. "I'll throw in a baked potato for you, too."

Dinner turned out pretty well, if I do say so myself. We took our meal to the coffee table in the living room and sat down on the futon.

"Do you like game shows?" I asked, turning on the television.

"Sure," she replied.

"I found this game show that I've never seen before," I told her. "It's pretty good."

"*Chances Are?*" she asked.

"Yeah," I said, and I realized that she'd been sequestered in her bedroom every evening listening to me watch it. "Do you like it?"

"Yes," she nodded. "It's brilliant."

We watched quietly until the first commercial break. That was when I told her, as nonchalantly as I could, "I'm getting a different couch tomorrow."

"You are?"

"Yeah," I nodded, spearing a wedge of tomato onto the end of my fork. I pointed down at the futon. "I hate this thing . . . it's really uncomfortable."

I put the tomato into my mouth.

"Oh," she said, nodding back.

I chewed and swallowed.

"I'm going to get rid of it," I said, wiping my mouth, "unless you want it or something."

We looked at each other for a long moment until I got really uncomfortable and went back to my salad.

"Has anyone ever told you that you're a terrible liar?" she asked.

I looked back up at her.

"I don't need charity," she said.

"It's not charity," I protested. "Can't I buy a new couch if I want?"

"Was it on sale like the ribeyes were?"

I glanced down at my plate.

"You're a terrible liar," she reiterated.

"I know," I sighed, looking back at her.

"I really appreciate what you're trying to do," she said gently, "but I'm okay."

"You're *not* okay," I protested. "You shouldn't be sleeping on the floor and eating ramen noodles every day."

"I don't mind," she assured me.

"*I* mind!"

Now it was her turn to sigh.

"Marco–"

"Look," I interrupted. "I've already ordered it, it's coming tomorrow . . . just *take* the futon."

She looked at me for a long moment.

"I *want* you to take it," I said. "Please?"

She finally gave me a little nod.

"Good," I said, satisfied. "Now eat your steak."

"Thank you," she said quietly, looking down at her plate and picking up her knife.

"You're welcome."

"I'll pay you back as soon as I get on my feet."

"I don't want you to pay me back."

She was quiet again for a minute and then finally asked, "Can I at least do the dishes tonight?"

I looked her dead in the eye and smiled.

"If you'll do the dishes, I'll cook dinner for you every single night."

~ ~ ~

I DON'T KNOW if Josette was tired of eating ramen noodles or if she believed me when I told her that I really did hate doing the dishes, but whatever the reason, the two of us started eating together every night after that, and on the third or fourth evening, she started helping me cook each evening too. This might have been because she thought my cooking needed help, or it might have been because she thought I shouldn't be handling knives and hot pans when I didn't have any fingers. I could tell she worried about me whenever I did, but it didn't take too long for her to realize that I did okay (and that if I wasn't a great cook, it wasn't because of my hands).

One evening, as I was using a small paring knife to peel garlic, I noticed her watching me curiously.

"What?" I asked, glancing at her.

"Nothing," she said, shaking her head. "I just . . ."

"What?"

She shrugged, then admitted, "I just think it's neat the way you can do so much stuff."

"I can do pretty much whatever I want." I nodded. "My parents never let me use my hands as an excuse for anything, so I pretty much had to figure out how to get things done."

"What happened?"

"To my hands?"

She nodded.

"I was born this way," I said, rinsing off the knife.

"Oh."

She didn't ask anything about my scar and I had almost convinced myself that my moustache covered it completely up, so I didn't tell her that I'd been born that way, too.

"I hope you don't think it's rude that I asked," she said.

"No. Not at all," I replied honestly. Then I looked at her and said, "Do you mind if I ask you something about *your* hands?"

"My hands?" she asked in surprise.

I nodded.

"What?"

I pointed with the tip of my knife to a pale band around the ring finger of her left hand.

"What's up with that?" I asked.

"Oh," she said, lowering her eyes.

"You don't have to tell me if you don't want to," I said hastily, already sorry that I'd asked.

"No," she said, shaking her head. "It's okay. I used to wear a ring, that's all."

"Well, I had *that* much figured," I said dryly.

She glanced at me.

"I was married," she finally explained, shrugging slightly. "Now we're separated."

I'd pretty much had that figured too, but she obviously didn't want to talk about it so I let it drop with a simple, "Oh. I'm sorry."

"Yeah," she nodded. "Thanks."

Josette and I continued timing dinner so that we could eat while watching *Chances Are*. Before long we were keeping score, competing against one another to see who could shout out the correct answer first. I'd thought Bizzy was competitive, but she was nothing compared to Josette.

A week or so after we had asked each other about our hands, the two of us were eating burgers on the couch when Wally Fletcher asked a contestant for the name of a beef dish that was made with a mashed potato crust on top.

"Shepherd's pie!" I called out confidently.

"Cottage pie," Josette said at the same time.

Wally proclaimed that Josette was right, and I stared at the TV in dismay.

"Shepherd's pie is made with *lamb*," Josette informed me.

"You can make it with beef, too," I insisted, looking at her. "My mom always makes it with beef."

"Then she's making Cottage Pie."

I pulled out my phone and searched the Internet just long enough to determine that she was right, and then I spent the rest of the evening sulking.

The next morning I called Mom.

"Will you send me your shepherd's pie recipe?" I asked when she answered.

"I'm not home," she reminded me. "We're visiting Grace."

"Well, I need you to send it to me," I said. "I tried to download one but it has carrots in it instead of peas, and then I just looked up another one and it has mushrooms in it."

"So?"

"So," I said, "you never put mushrooms in it."

"Then don't put mushrooms in it."

"But I want it to taste like *yours*," I complained. "There's about fifty-thousand recipes out there and I don't know which one is yours."

"Feeling homesick?" she asked.

"Something like that."

She started rattling off a list of ingredients and steps.

"Whoa, whoa, whoa," I said. "I'm driving and I can't write it down right now. Can you send it to me?"

"Sure," she agreed. "I'll write it down and get it in tomorrow's mail."

"No, I want to make it tonight," I said. "Can you email it to me?"

"Email it?"

"Please?"

"Your dad's not even here," she said worriedly. "Andrew got them a reservation for eighteen holes at Pebble Beach and they just left a little bit ago." (Andrew was the fiancé that Grace had somehow managed to snag.)

"Grace has a computer, Mom," I said patiently. "She can help you do it."

"Okay," Mom agreed. "I'll see what I can do."

"Thanks, Mom," I said. "I love you."

By the time Josette walked in the door late that afternoon, I was sliding a casserole dish into the oven.

"Get ready to have the best thing you've ever eaten in your entire life," I told her.

"Cottage pie or shepherd's pie?"

"You'll just have to wait and see."

She smiled.

"Need any help?" she asked.

"Nope. I've got everything under control."

"Okay," she nodded. "I'm going to go change and I'll be out in a minute."

"Okay," I nodded back.

She was actually gone a lot longer than a minute, and what brought her out was the sound of the smoke alarm.

"What's going on?" she shouted over the din.

"I don't know!" I cried. I was already reaching into the oven with potholders and pulling the casserole dish out as smoke billowed into the kitchen. The top potato layer was completely black, burned beyond recognition.

"What did you *do*?"

"Nothing!" I said, backing away from the stove and fanning it with a potholder. Josette grabbed a magazine and began waving it in front of the smoke detector.

I turned on the hood fan and Josette started opening windows, but the air was so thick with smoke that we soon retreated, coughing, to the front porch.

"What in the *world* happened?" she asked after our coughing had subsided.

"I don't know," I said once more. "I was just following the directions and doing what they told me to do."

"How long was it in there?"

"Only about five minutes."

"At what temperature?"

"High."

"You had it on *broil*?"

"Yeah," I nodded. "It said 'Top rack. Broil on high for fifteen minutes'."

She stared at me in disbelief for a moment.

"Are you sure that's what it said?"

"Positive."

Now she looked at me doubtfully.

"That's what it said," I insisted, pulling my phone out to show her the email.

She took it from me and peered at it intently, her eyes narrowing after a moment.

"This can't be right, Marco," she said, handing me back my phone.

"What do you mean?"

"I mean," she explained, "that I can't think of a single thing you can broil on high on the top rack for *fifteen* minutes without burning it to a crisp."

"But that's what my mom does," I said slowly.

"I don't think so," she said, shaking her head, and all of a sudden it clicked.

"Grace . . ." I muttered.

"What?"

"Grace!" I said louder. "It was GRACE!"

"What was Grace?"

"That *WITCH*!!" I yelled and Josette's eyes got wide *really* wide (because "witch" isn't at all what I said).

I picked up one of my new wrought-iron chairs from the front porch and heaved it toward the driveway with all my might. The chair clanged and bounced against the pavement, missing my car by inches. I turned around and slammed my hand against the doorframe.

"Who's Grace?" Josette finally dared to ask.

"My stupid sister!" I shouted.

"What does she have to do with anything?"

"My mom sent me this recipe," I explained to Josette, waving my phone at her. "She's the most technologically illiterate person on the face of this planet. She can barely operate her phone. She would have had to have Grace help her send it – it came *from* Grace. My mom wouldn't have made a mistake like that, but Grace . . . Oh my gosh. WHAT A *WITCH!*"

(Again, not at all what I said, and again with another chair into the driveway. Now I had a matched set.)

Josette bit her lip and watched as I turned around, closed my eyes and banged my forehead against the storm door.

"I hate her," I said.

Bang.

"I hate her. I hate her. I HATE her."

Bang. Bang. Bang.

"Marco," Josette said softly, laying a hand gently on my shoulder. "Why don't we go get a pizza and let the smell get out of the house and then I'll help you get things cleaned up when we get back?"

"I'm not hungry," I said, giving my head one more good whack against the door.

"I am," she said. "I'm starving. All I had for lunch was some celery."

I rolled my forehead against the door to look at her sideways.

"I packed you leftovers today."

"I know," she said, smiling at me. "But I really am hungry. Come on. You're not going to make me take the bus at night and eat all by myself, are you?"

She knew she had me.

I looked at her for a moment and sighed before going back into the smoky house to get my keys.

It was almost midnight in Monterey, but I didn't care. I called Mom on my way to the pizzeria and gave her an earful. When I hung up, I glanced at Josette and was surprised to see her shoulders shaking, her hand covering her mouth.

"What's so funny?"

"I can't believe you actually just called your mom and dobbed on your sister!"

I had never heard the word *dobbed* before. I had also never heard Josette laugh.

"Dobbed?"

"You know," she said. "You told on her . . . tattled."

I looked at her uncertainly.

"What's your mom going to do," she continued on, still laughing. "Ground her? Put her in a time-out?"

I didn't answer.

"You know, Marco," she said, not laughing quite as much but definitely still laughing. "You reacted *exactly* the way Grace wanted you too. You played right into her hands."

"What was I supposed to do?" I asked angrily. "Ignore it?"

"Yes," she agreed, nodding. "That, or – if you really wanted to get back at her – you should have called your mom and thanked her for the recipe and told her that it turned out brilliantly. *That* would have made Grace mad."

I thought about that for a minute and then I answered, "I'm a terrible liar, remember?"

"I remember," Josette said, and she laughed again.

~ ~ ~

THE FOLLOWING SUNDAY, Josette invited me to go to church with her. This might have been because it was starting to feel like the two of us were becoming friends, or it might have been because my foul mouth had convinced her that I needed to hear the Word of God.

I had actually been trying different churches every weekend since I'd arrived in Australia, but I hadn't found anything that had tripped my trigger yet, so when she asked me if I wanted to go with her, I said sure, and I offered to drive.

"I usually go to Sunday School, too," she said hesitantly.

"That's fine," I answered.

As soon as we arrived at Hope Springs the following Sunday, I was pretty confident that this church wasn't going to trip my trigger either. Everyone in the Sunday School class that Josette belonged to seemed to be a lot more . . . *mature* than I was (read: gray hair, bifocals, hearing aids, and dentures). I couldn't begin to imagine for the life of me why she had joined a class where no one was even remotely close to her own age, but they all welcomed me with such open arms and seemed so genuinely glad to have me with them that I knew I was going to feel forever guilty if I didn't come back every Sunday for the rest of my life (or at least for the rest of theirs). It was clear that they loved Josette, too, hugging her and kissing her on the cheek as she greeted each one of them by name and introduced me to them.

Then we sat down for the lesson, and after that I knew for sure that I would keep coming back.

One day in October I came home to find Josette's purse on the table, but the house empty. Her door was open, her futon neatly made, but she was nowhere to be found. She wouldn't have taken the bus without her purse and she wouldn't have gone for a walk without locking the front door . . .

I found her in my tiny backyard.

"What are you doing?" I asked, stepping out onto the back stoop.

She looked back at me and smiled.

"Getting something for dinner," she grinned.

I walked toward her. She was standing in front of a small tree and reaching to pluck some kind of fruit from it. The fruit was red and about the size of a plum, and she dropped each one that she picked into the front of her t-shirt, which she was holding out in front of her as if it were a basket.

"What are those?" I asked.

"Quandongs."

"Quandongs?"

She nodded.

"You're kidding, right?"

She giggled.

"Are you sure they're edible?" I asked worriedly.

"Of course I'm sure," she said, laughing again and handing me one. "Try it."

I took a bite and my teeth sliced through a thin layer of fruit before hitting something hard.

"You could have told me it had a pit," I complained.

"It's a nut," she corrected.

"If I cracked a tooth does it really matter what it's called?"

"Sorry," she smiled.

"I don't think you are . . ."

"And I don't think you cracked a tooth," she said, laughing.

"It tastes like a peach," I told her, licking my lips.

"Yes," she agreed. "Some people call it a wild peach."

"That sounds a whole lot better than *quandong*," I said. She giggled again and I asked, "What are you going to do with them?"

"Make a pie."

"I like pie," I smiled.

"You've got a muntrie bush right over there," she said, pointing to the opposite corner of the yard. "I don't think they usually do great this far south, but if it gets any fruit after Christmas, I'll make you a muntrie pie too."

"What are muntries?"

"Ummm," she thought for a moment. "They kind of look like blueberries, but they taste like spicy apples."

"I've practically got an orchard here," I observed, looking around my backyard. She giggled yet again.

I looked at her suspiciously.

"What?" she asked.

"You're in an *awfully* good mood today," I observed. She hardly ever laughed. I could probably count on one hand . . . well, no I couldn't, but you know what I mean.

She smiled some more and nodded.

"What's up?"

"I got a scholarship," she said, now positively grinning from ear to ear.

"Really?"

"Yes," she nodded. "I'm going to be able to start school after Christmas!"

"Cool."

She nodded and smiled even wider.

"What are you going to take?"

"I want to major in literature."

"Now there's a field that's teeming with job opportunities," I said sarcastically.

She smirked at me.

"I'm going to go on and get my master's degree and maybe even my doctorate, thank you very much."

"And then what are you going to do?"

"I'm going to be a librarian."

"Cool," I said again, nodding my approval.

"When I was little," she went on, "my mum used to take me to the main library in Montreal and I would–"

"Montreal?" I interrupted.

"Uh-huh . . ."

"Canada?"

"Is there another Montreal?" she asked, raising any eyebrow.

"What were you doing in Montreal?"

"I lived there until I was fourteen," she said.

"Seriously?" I asked excitedly. "That's where my girlfriend lives!"

"What part?"

"Well, her family actually lives in Peterborough, but she went to school at UM. I used to go there to see her all the time when I was at Princeton."

"Then you weren't very far from where my grandparents live."

"Do you visit them much?" I asked, now using my own shirt as a basket to hold fruit because hers was getting pretty full.

"No," she said, shaking her head. "Never."

"Oh."

"It's my mum's parents," she explained. "My dad kind of had a falling out with them after Mum died."

"Oh," I said again.

"She died when I was thirteen," Josette said. "She got stomach cancer and they tried all these alternative treatments and stuff, but she didn't make it. Her parents pretty much blamed my dad. They said if he'd taken her to a real doctor she probably would have lived."

I looked at her.

"They were probably right," she said, shrugging and putting a quandong in my shirt. "My parents didn't always make the best decisions. They were kind of ummm . . ." She hesitated. "Free spirits?" she finally suggested. "Hippies?"

I gave her a little smile.

"Come on," she said, motioning toward the house. "We've got enough. Let's go on in."

We headed toward the house.

"My dad got into this huge fight with her parents after she died," she went on. "They threatened to sue for custody of me and he told them that if they did, he'd move me to the other side of the world so that they'd never see me again."

I looked at her, waiting for her to continue.

"They didn't back down," she said, shrugging her shoulders. "So he flew me to Perth, bought a yacht, and we started homeschooling."

"You lived on a yacht?" I asked, holding the back door open for her.

"Yeah," she said. "For almost three years, until he met Clarissa and bought a little house."

"How'd you wind up here?" I asked. (Perth was on the other side of the continent and over two thousand miles away.)

She smiled at me one more time and headed into the kitchen.

"That's a story for another day," she said.

Josette made the pie while I worked on the rest of dinner. She told me how her mother had instilled in her a deep love of reading at an early age, but how she had almost regretted doing so by the time Josette finished elementary school.

"I always had my nose stuck in a book," Josette remembered, holding a measuring cup up in front of her face. She put a hand on one hip and bit her lip in concentration as she studied the numbers on the glass, finally deciding that she had the right amount of water. She gave me a little smile. "Mum worried that she'd created a monster."

I smiled back.

"She said that people who read too much are just trying to escape the realities of life," Josette said, pouring the water into a mixing bowl.

"Were you?"

"I don't know," she shrugged, beginning to stir. "Maybe. But isn't it better to escape by reading than by smoking pot all day?"

"Probably."

She shook her head and rolled her eyes.

"Anyway," she said. "I still love to read. Give me a rainy day and something to read by C.S. Lewis or Jane Austen and I'm a happy camper."

"Ugh," I said. "I hate Jane Austen."

She looked at me as if I'd just grown a second head.

"How can you hate Jane Austen?" she asked in disbelief.

"Umm, let's see," I said, looking up at the ceiling with my hand on my chin as if I were thinking hard. "You have to read everything about five times to even *begin* to understand what she's talking about, she writes sentences that are longer than normal people's paragraphs, her characters are silly, her plots are boring, the endings are ridiculous . . ."

I glanced at Josette, wondering if I should continue. She was still staring at me with her mouth open.

"It does take some time to get used to her," she finally admitted.

"I don't have that much time."

"She's a wonderful writer–"

"She's *not* a wonderful writer," I argued. "The woman doesn't know when to use a period! I had to read some stupid book of hers when I was in high school and–"

"Which one?"

"I don't know," I said. "I've blocked it from my memory."

"*Pride and Prejudice*?"

"No."

"*Sense and Sensibility*?"

"That's it."

"I like that one," she smiled.

"She had one sentence in there that was so long that I actually counted how many words it had."

"How many did it have?"

"I don't know – like a hundred and twenty-something?"

Josette laughed and I shook my head.

"My favorite is *Persuasion*," she said.

"Never heard of it."

"You should give it a try sometime."

"Not gonna happen."

Josette smiled again and then, with a gleam in her eye, asked, "Do you want to see something?"

"Sure," I shrugged.

She set down the wooden spoon she had been stirring with and went into her bedroom, emerging a moment later with a small set of light-blue books. There were five of them. They were all by Jane Austen and obviously quite old.

"My mum got me these," she said.

"I thought you said she thought you already read too much."

"That's one of the reasons they're so special to me," she said, smiling. "She knew how much they meant to me so she got them for me anyway."

I looked at them again.

"Where's *Persuasion*?" I asked dramatically. "I thought it was your favorite."

"She found these at an antique shop," Josette explained. "That one was missing."

"Well, why don't you get one?"

"Trust me," she laughed. "If I could, I would, but I can't. This set is very collectible, and quite out of my price range."

"You can't have an incomplete set," I frowned.

"Feel free to complete it for me any time you want," she said, and she laughed one more time.

~ ~ ~

AS IF I wasn't going to take her up on that.

I snuck into Josette's room while she was at work one day and copied down the name of the publishing house and the copyright dates. It wasn't too hard to find a copy of the missing book online, and it really wasn't all that expensive (at least not when you have a paid internship and your parents are paying most of your bills). When it arrived in the mail a week later, I really wanted to give it to her right away, but I forced myself to tuck it into the back of my closet to save for Christmas.

By this point, Josette and I were already cooking and eating and going to church together, but after the day she made us quandong pie we started doing other stuff together, too. We went out to eat sometimes or went to the movies, and a few times we even went to St. Kilda together. Sometimes we shopped, and sometimes we walked along the beach and talked.

I learned that Josette had been stung by a Portuguese man-of-war the very first time she swam in the Indian Ocean – right after her father had moved them to Perth. I learned that Perth and Montreal were near antipodes of one another – two diametrically opposed points on a sphere. I learned that this was how she had wound up in Australia in the first place – because her father had literally spun a globe to make good on his threat to "move Josie clear to the other side of the world."

I learned that I could call her Josie.

Josette wasn't the roommate I had once envisioned myself playing Frisbee with . . . she wasn't the girlfriend I was still hoping would decide to move to Melbourne to be with me . . . she wasn't the brother I was anxiously awaiting a visit from in the spring . . .

But things were a lot nicer in Australia once I had a friend to do things with.

~ ~ ~

ONE DAY I came down with a bad cold, and when Josette found out that I was sick, she told me that she had just the thing to make me feel better. While I sat on the couch, she took a loaf of bread from the top of the fridge and opened the bag, pulling out two slices and dropping them into the toaster.

After the bread popped up, she worked away for a few minutes and soon brought me a plate with two pieces of toast, each covered with a brown paste.

"That's not Vegemite, is it?" I asked unhappily.

"You don't like Vegemite?"

I shook my head.

"Have you ever tried it?" she asked suspiciously.

"I bought some as soon as I moved here," I insisted. "I opened the jar, smelled it, and I threw it away."

She tipped her head at me disapprovingly.

"You can't decide if you like something or not by smelling it," she said. "This is just the thing to eat when you're not feeling well. Take a few bites and see if it doesn't make you feel better."

I was pretty sure that it wasn't going to, but I obediently reached for a piece of toast and sniffed at it tentatively.

"Quit *smelling* it," she scolded. "Try it."

"My mom used to make me chicken noodle soup when I was sick," I said pitifully.

"Mine did, too," she said. "But this is what we have right now. Try it."

I reluctantly took a little nibble.

"All you got was bread," she accused.

I took another bite and gagged.

"Oh, that's gross."

"Give it to me," she said disgustedly, taking the toast out of my hand. She took a bite and I gagged again.

"You don't know what you're missing," she said after she swallowed.

Meanwhile, graduate school was going great. I was taking classes and working as a TA in an undergraduate physics lab, but most of my time was spent in my internship, doing actual research, which I really loved.

I called Bizzy almost every day. Apparently she was enjoying things at Curtis as much as I was enjoying things at Melbourne, and she told me that she was applying to travel to South America for a few weeks to study El Sistema, a music program in Venezuela that worked with impoverished children. She told me that her parents were going to take her to Italy over Christmas break (which ticked me off a bit because her trip was at the same time that I was going to be back in the States), but she placated me by assuring me that we would get to see each other in California over the summer. She was going to be one of Grace's bridesmaids and she promised to stay several extra days after the wedding so that we could spend some time together.

I didn't really want to wait that long to see her, but it was better than nothing, and it wasn't as if there was anything I could do about it anyway.

As the upside-down Australian days grew longer and warmer, I grew anxious to see my family. I found out that Josette was going to be spending Christmas all alone, however, and that really bothered me (no matter how many times she tried to convince me that she was going to be happy as a clam while I was gone because she had a whole list of books that she wanted to read).

There wasn't anything I could do about that, either, however, so the day before I was set to fly out to see my family, I handed her the copy of *Persuasion* I'd bought for her and said, "Here . . . add this to your reading list."

She gently tore the wrapping paper off and stared at the cover of the book that she was holding in her hands.

"I can't believe you got this for me," she whispered, seemingly in awe. "You shouldn't have done that."

"It was no big deal," I said. "Merry Christmas."

She gawked at it for another moment and then said, "Thank you," before adding, "I've got something for you, too."

"Really?"

She nodded and went into her bedroom. When she emerged, she was carrying three gift bags, and she set them down on the couch.

"What in the world is all that?" I asked.

"Stuff for your trip!" she answered, smiling proudly. "This one," she explained, holding up the biggest bag, "is for you to share with your family. It's peppermint bark and cheese straws and stuff like that that'll keep for a while so you can pack it in your suitcase.

"This one," she said, holding up the next bag, which was quite a bit smaller, "is stuff that I *think* they'll let you carry on board, but I'm not positive – you might have to throw it away when you get to security. It's stuff for you to eat on the plane . . . some Anzac biscuits and chocolate chip cookies and stuff.

"And this one," she finished, holding up the third bag, "you have to eat tonight."

I peered down into the bag to see a brown lump of something that looked suspiciously like fruitcake.

"What's that?"

"Christmas pudding," she said. "It's a traditional Australian recipe. It's got butter and brown sugar and currants and almonds and–"

"Do I have to share?" I interrupted.

"Nope," she said. "It's your Christmas present. You can eat the whole thing all by yourself if you want."

I smiled at her.

"But if you do," she said, "I hope you get sick as a dog."

Beginning on the plane ride, Josette's stash of food was devoured quickly. Like Josette had instructed, I shared a lot of it with my family, but when Mom asked where the roasted quandong nuts and homemade hot cocoa mix had come from, I told her that a woman from the university had made it for me. (This was not a total lie. Josette *was* a woman and she *was* officially from the university now that she was enrolled as a freshman and scheduled to start classes at the end of February.) Somehow I didn't think Mom was going to handle it too well if she found out that my roommate was a female, so I didn't elaborate any more than I had to and was thankful when Grace started grumbling about how I had eaten all of the fudge.

For Christmas, I had bought Mom an Australian black opal pendant. Dad and Dorito got Wallabies rugby jerseys, and I gave my younger nieces didgeridoos, which are traditional Australian wind instruments. It only took a few minutes of listening to *those* on Christmas morning for me to begin to second-guess that decision, but at least my older nieces didn't break any windows or anything with their boomerangs and my sisters seemed to like their wool scarves, compliments of some Australian sheep.

Dorito's in-laws wanted to have all of their granddaughters to themselves for a few days, which meant that Dorito and his wife Maria and I got to go away by ourselves for two nights, skiing. I told Dorito all about everything there was to do in and around Melbourne, and we started making plans for his upcoming visit.

I could hardly wait.

~ ~ ~

WHEN I GOT back to Australia, Josette led me out into our tiny backyard to show me the muntrie bush. It was covered with little green berries that she assured me would ripen soon, and she promised me again that she would make me a muntrie pie.

She wound up being so busy once school started a few weeks later, however, that I wondered whether she would actually have time to make me a pie once the berries ripened. Although she scaled back some on her hours at the electronics store where she was a cashier so she would have more time for her classes, she obtained a work-study position at the main library on campus, and it seemed that she wound up working more than ever.

She wasn't home much in the evenings anymore (and when she was, she was usually busy either reading or studying), but she still almost always ate dinner with me while we watched *Chances Are*, and she still did the dishes for me every night. She had recorded every episode that I'd missed while I was gone over Christmas, but we never seemed to have the chance to watch anything except for the current episodes because she was too busy to watch the older ones.

She seemed happy though.

She might have had very little spare time now that she was back in school, and it still might have been a rare thing to hear her laugh, but at least she smiled more than she ever had.

~ ~ ~

ONE MORNING, WHILE I was still asleep, my phone vibrated. I looked at the screen, saw that it was Dad, and answered extra groggily to make sure that he knew that he'd woken me up. When he didn't apologize though, and instead began by saying, "I have some bad news, Marco," I suddenly wasn't groggy anymore.

He had been having some trouble with his memory.
He and Mom were in the States.
He had gone to see a specialist at the Mayo Clinic.
He had been diagnosed with early-onset Alzheimer's.
He was on some medicine that was hopefully going to help.
He was fifty-four years old.

I was speechless for a moment until I finally told him, "I'm going to come home."
"For what?"
"To be with you!" I exclaimed. "To help you!"
"Help me what?"
I couldn't say anything.
"Marco, everything's fine right now," Dad insisted. "There's no need for you to come home."
"I *want* to come home," I said quietly.
"Well, I *don't* want you to come home," he persisted. "You've worked way too hard to get where you are."
"I want to come home," I said again, trying very hard not to cry.
"Marco," he insisted, "listen to me. You're coming home for the wedding in just a few months. See how things are then, okay? If you get here and you decide you want to stay home

then you can, but *please* finish out the semester. Please promise me that you won't let this stop you."

I couldn't speak.

"Marco?"

I still couldn't.

"Marco?"

"What?" I managed to ask after a moment.

"What you're doing makes me so proud," he said quietly. "Don't quit now, just because of this."

I lost it.

"Here," I heard my mom say. "Let me talk to him."

Mom came on and tried to calm me down over all my sobbing, but there wasn't really anything she could do. Finally I managed to pull myself together long enough so that she'd be able to hang up in good conscience, but as soon as she did I broke down again.

It was then that I became aware of the fact that Josette was next to me with her hand on my back. She had obviously heard me crying and let herself into my room. I glanced up at her in despair.

"What happened?" she asked gently, sitting down next to me on my bed. And I told her everything.

"I'm so sorry, Marco," she said when I finished, her hand still on my back.

I sat there with my face buried in my hands and thought about what a great dad he was and how he had taken me home from that orphanage and done everything that he could for me to let me have the best life possible. Not just me, but my brother and sisters too. All of us.

"How can this be happening?" I cried.

Josette didn't answer but gently rubbed my shoulder.

"He is such a good person," I said, looking up at her. "He's the best person I've ever known."

She nodded at me.

"When I was little," I told her, "he always used to pack my lunch to take to school because I wouldn't eat what they had at the cafeteria."

She nodded again.

"And one day I didn't eat my sandwich," I said, "and he asked me why and I told him that there was too much jelly on it . . . it had soaked through the bread and it was all soggy . . . you know?"

I was fully aware that I was babbling, but it felt really good to be talking about him. She looked at me understandingly.

"And so then he started putting just a little bit of jelly on it after that so I'd eat them, but one day on a Saturday he made one for me and I told him it didn't have enough jelly on it and he said, 'I thought you didn't want a lot of jelly on it', and I told him it only soaked through if it sat around in my lunch bag all day but I liked a lot of jelly if I was going to get to eat it right away . . ."

She probably thought I was insane, but she just kept nodding and looking at me like I was making perfect sense, so I kept going.

"He totally got it," I said, "and he always did it right after that. He was the best dad . . ."

I started crying again.

Josette sat there like that with me for a long time with her arm around me, just listening. I talked about the day he had stopped by my school when I was little and told them I had a doctor's appointment just so that he could take me fishing, and I told her about how he had spent hours with me in the backyard, shooting the soccer ball at a full-sized goal he'd set up so that I could practice blocking shots and about how he'd flown me to Boston so I could finally have a moustache. As that story was coming out of my mouth I couldn't believe I was sitting there telling Josette that I'd had a cleft palate and facial hair transplant, but I was too upset to be embarrassed and she didn't change the look on her face at all or act like she minded, so I kept on going.

When I eventually started running out of steam, I took a long, jagged breath. Josette rubbed my back and asked me if she could get me anything. I shook my head.

"Have you had breakfast?"

"I can't keep anything down," I said, shaking my head.

"You need to eat something," she insisted. She stood up and headed out of my room. "I know something that will make you feel better."

I looked at the clock on my nightstand.

"You're late for work," I called after her, standing up and following her.

"It's okay," she assured me.

"No it's not," I said. "You need to get to the library."

"It's okay," she said again. "I'll call Brenda and tell her I can't make it."

"You just started working there," I argued. "You can't skip out already."

"It'll be fine," she promised. "Brenda's nice."

I stopped arguing because I didn't really want to be alone. I sat down on the couch, staring at the darkened TV.

"What are you making?" I asked when I heard her opening a cupboard.

"Vegemite."

I turned to look at her, alarmed, and she smiled at me.

"Just wait and see," she said gently with another smile.

In a few minutes she brought a bowl in and put it down in front of me.

Chicken noodle soup.

I looked down at it and teared up again.

Josette sat down beside me and started rubbing her hand across my back once more.

She stayed quiet.

I knew she was waiting to see if I wanted to talk anymore but I didn't. I picked up the remote to turn on the TV. I ate my soup and the two of us sat together on the couch for the entire day.

We watched every single episode of *Chances Are* that she had recorded while I'd been gone over Christmas.

~ ~ ~

DORITO CALLED ME the next morning and I talked with him for a long time. The sense of impending doom that I'd felt since the day before lifted a bit, and he wrapped up our conversation by telling me that he loved me and reminded me that he'd see me in a few weeks.

After that, Dad called me too, and I felt even better after talking to him for a second time. He sounded completely like himself and so normal that I began to convince myself that I still had a long time left with him. When I hung up the phone that time, I felt good enough to get dressed and go to the lab.

I couldn't wait to see Dorito.

I had to battle with Josette about where he was going to sleep when he arrived as she insisted that she was going to go to a hotel, but I knew she couldn't really afford to do that, and I also knew that she wouldn't be comfortable letting me pay for it. She talked about asking her boss Brenda if she could stay at her house, but I finally convinced her that I wanted to rent a rollaway bed to put in my bedroom so that Dorito and I could lay awake at night and talk like we had done all the time when we were younger.

She eyed me suspiciously.

"What?" I asked.

"I'm trying to figure out if you're lying or not," she said.

"I'm getting better at it, aren't I?" I grinned. She shook her head in mock disgust, but I knew I had convinced her to stay.

Once Dorito arrived and had been advised of the sleeping arrangements, Josette said, "Marco tells me that you're used to sharing a room with him."

82

Dorito looked at me in confusion.

"I *knew* you were lying," she muttered.

"*Muñeco*," Dorito gasped in mock dismay. "You lied?"

"We used to share a room whenever we went to Grandma and Grandpa's," I argued.

"This is true," he conceded, giving Josette a shrug.

"*Muñeco?*" Josette said questioningly.

Dorito started to open his mouth to explain, but I elbowed him in the ribs as hard as I could.

"Don't you need to get to class?" I asked her.

She looked at her watch.

"I suppose I should get going," she admitted, but she had a glint in her eye and I knew she wasn't going to let it drop.

As soon as Josette was out the door, Dorito turned to me with raised eyebrows. "Wow," he said. "How'd you manage to pull that off?"

"Pull what off?"

"Getting *her*," he said, jabbing his thumb toward the door for emphasis, "for a roommate?"

"She just needed a place to stay," I said, shrugging. "It's no big deal."

"Uh-huh."

"It's not!" I insisted. "I've already got a girlfriend, in case you've forgotten."

"And does Bizzy know about her?"

"Yes."

"I bet she doesn't know what she *looks* like," he said.

"Of course she doesn't," I snapped. "She's blind!"

"Yeah," he agreed, "but I bet you didn't bother to fill her in."

"There's nothing to 'fill her in' on. She's not even all that . . ."

My voice faded off.

"Okay, fine," I finally said. "She's pretty. Big deal."

Dorito bit back a smile and shook his head.

"Do Mom and Dad know about her?" he asked.

"Not exactly . . ."

"Wow. I can't believe you've turned into such a liar," Dorito said, not bothering to suppress his smile this time.

"I didn't *lie* to anybody," I protested. "I've just kind of avoided the subject."

"There's no way Mom hasn't grilled you about your roommate," he argued.

"Well, no," I admitted. "I just kept it kind of vague." I coughed into my hand and then muttered, "And I might have referred to her as 'Jo'."

He laughed out loud.

"I didn't know you had it in you," he said, shaking his head with a grin on his face. "Oh, man, are you ever gonna get it! They're coming to visit in like a month!"

"I know," I sighed. "What should I do?"

"I don't know," Dorito said, shaking a finger at me in reprimand. "This is why you're never supposed to lie."

"Oh, right," I said, shoving him. "Like you never lie!"

"I never said that," he admitted, laughing again, "but I'm a whole lot better at it than you are!"

I glared at him.

"What were you thinking, Marco?" he asked, a little more seriously.

"I don't know," I said helplessly. "It's really *not* that big of a deal!"

"Yeah," he laughed. "Tell that to Mom."

"I'm almost twenty-three years old," I reminded him.

"They still paying your rent and stuff?" he asked.

I sighed once more.

"What should I do?" I asked again. "Should I tell them now so they have a chance to get over it before they get here?"

"Oh, no," he replied adamantly, shaking his head. "It's too late for that. Your best bet is to wait until they get here and just play dumb. Maybe you'll get lucky and they won't want to make a big scene in front of her."

Dorito had been working Mom and Dad a whole lot longer than I had . . .

I nodded and decided to take his advice.

By the time Mom and Dad arrived, however, I was really second-guessing that decision. I picked them up at Tullamarine Airport, giving them both (but especially Dad) extra-long hugs. I was really glad to see them and particularly relieved that Dad seemed to be doing well, but I was still so worried about how they were going to react to finding out about Josette that by the time we'd loaded their luggage into my car, driven to the house, and pulled into the driveway, I was sweating bullets.

I popped the trunk and hurried out of the car, immediately busying myself with the two largest suitcases they'd brought. My throat was so dry I could barely speak, but when I reached the top step of the porch I managed to turn around and say to them very quickly, "I may have forgotten to mention to you that my roommate is a female." Then I turned back around just as quickly and pushed the front door open without waiting for their reaction.

Even though I had my back to them, I knew that Mom and Dad were staring at each other in shock, but – just as Dorito had predicted – they were too polite to make a scene in front of Josette. Instead, they stepped into the living room and stood before her with their mouths slightly open, shooting furtive glances at one another but mustering up the manners to reach out and shake her hand.

To my surprise, I noticed that Josette was staring right back at them with her own mouth slightly open, shooting furtive glances at me. I couldn't imagine what *her* problem was, but then I looked at my parents again . . .

My very *white* parents.

"Oh," I said to Josette, as understanding dawned on me. "I may have forgotten to mention to you that I was adopted."

Interestingly enough, Mom took to Josette right off. She believed me when I told her that nothing was going on between the two of us, and she really seemed to like Josette. As a matter of fact, sometimes it felt as if Mom was more interested in talking with Josette than she was with me. The two of them worked on dinner together on the nights that we didn't go out, they went shopping together several times, and one day Mom even treated Josette to a pedicure. They came home from that excursion laughing and giggling and showing off their toenails, and then Mom made Dad help her find a bunch of baby pictures and videos of me to show Josette.

There I was with a big, gaping hole in my face, giving the camera the biggest smile I had because I didn't know any better.

"Oh, my gosh," Josette gasped, her hand flying to her mouth as she stared at the screen. "That is the cutest thing I've ever seen."

I thought I was going to die.

I don't know if Dad liked Josette or not, but he definitely had a problem with the fact that I was living with a woman. He let me know this the very second Josette and Mom took my car the first time to go shopping.

"You're not being smart," he told me.

I sighed. "Nothing is going on."

"That doesn't mean it's going to stay that way."

"I love Bizzy," I reminded him. "Nothing's going to happen between me and Josie. She's just a friend."

"Yeah," he said. "Your mom and I started out as friends too."

I rolled my eyes.

"Look," he said. "You may have the best of intentions here, but God designed us a certain way. We have hormones that–"

"You did *not* just say the word 'hormones' to me," I interrupted.

He looked at me.

"I am not having this conversation with you," I cried. "I'm twenty-three years old and I know all about hormones and everything else and I'm in love with Bizzy and nothing's going to happen between me and Josette. I know what I'm doing!"

"I know you *think* you know what you're doing–" he began, but I cut him off again.

"I *know* what I'm doing," I insisted.

He looked at me once more.

"Can you please not make a big deal out of this?" I begged. "I really was hoping that we could just have a nice time together while you're here."

That struck a chord. A chord that's easily struck in someone who has realized just how limited his days are. He looked at me for a moment and then nodded in silent agreement. I let out a sigh of relief.

"But I want you to promise me something," he said, obviously determined to get the last word in.

"What?" I sighed.

"Promise me that if anything *does* happen between the two of you that you won't keep living together. One of you needs to move out."

"Nothing's going to happen between the two of us," I insisted.

"Just promise me that if it does one of you will move out," he said again. "I'll pay more for your rent or whatever you need, but it's not a good idea for the two of you to live together under the same roof if you're . . . you know."

I didn't bother telling him again that nothing was going to happen between me and Josette and that I loved Bizzy and that he didn't need to worry about it. It was easier just to tell him what he wanted to hear.

"I promise," I nodded. "If Josie and I ever decide to start dating, I'll kick her right out."

Mom and Dad slept in my room while they were visiting and I slept on the couch, which was way too short for me. I was glad to get my bed back after they left, but that was the only thing good about having them gone. I missed them the instant they checked through security.

I think Josette knew that I was going to be feeling homesick once they left because when I got back from the airport she was making my favorite childhood meal of meatloaf and potato casserole.

"Your mom gave me the recipe," she explained kindly. Then she added with a wicked grin, "*Muñeco.*"

I rolled my eyes and she laughed one of her rare laughs.

"Why wouldn't you tell me about that?" she asked, still laughing. "It's so cute!"

"Because it's embarrassing!" I cried.

"But you were their little *Muñeco,*" she said in a baby voice. "Their little *doll.*"

I rolled my eyes again and shook my head, turning on my heel and stalking into my room.

I came back out when Josette called me for dinner. She didn't tease me anymore, but she still had a glint in her eye. We sat in front of the television and watched our show while we ate.

"This tastes great," I told her between bites of meatloaf and Wally Fletcher's questions. "Thank you."

"You're welcome."

The food and the familiarity of our routine comforted me and I felt grateful. She didn't call me *Muñeco* anymore, and I was grateful for that, too. By the first commercial break, I was three questions ahead of her and feeling almost happy.

But then Josette reached for the remote and muted the television.

"Can I talk to you about something?" she asked.

I was immediately worried by the seriousness of her voice.

"You're not moving out," I asked. "Are you?"

"No," she smiled.

"Good," I said. "Go ahead. Talk away."

"I wanted to talk to you about Grace."

"Unless it's about Grace," I said quickly, trying to snatch the remote out of her hand. "You can talk to me about anything except you moving out or about Grace."

"Marco . . ." She held the remote just out of my reach.

"Why are you trying to ruin a perfectly good meal?" I asked.

"Because I learned a lot about both of you when your parents were here and I think maybe I have an idea about why the two of you don't get along so well."

"Maybe it's because she's a *bi*–"

Josette shot her hand out and covered my mouth before I could finish that sentence.

"Will you just listen to me, please?" she asked.

I crossed my arms and sat back on the couch, suddenly no longer hungry.

"I'd rather talk about you moving out," I said.

"Thanks a lot!"

I glared at her.

"Say whatever you want to say and get it over with." I sulked.

"Okay." Josette nodded. "I think the reason she's so mean to you is because she's jealous of you."

"*Jealous* of me?" I asked, incredulous. "That's the stupidest thing I've ever heard in my entire life!"

"No, it's not," she insisted. "I've put a lot of thought into this and I really think that's what's going on."

I looked at her skeptically.

"Look," she said patiently. "Which one of you was adopted first?"

"She was."

"And how old was she when your parents brought you home?"

"I don't know," I shrugged. "I guess about four months old."

"How old were you when you had your surgery?"

"I had a lot of surgeries," I told her.

"Well, how old were you when you had them?"

I shrugged again. "I guess I had my first one when I was about six months old and I know I had one around the time I was about a year old."

"So she was about sixteen months old," Josette clarified. "And was that it?"

"No," I said. "I had to have surgery on my pharynx when I was in kindergarten and a bone graft when I was in fourth grade."

"Is that it?"

"Unless you count my moustache surgery," I said sheepishly.

"I count it," she replied seriously. "Grace might not have known exactly *what* you were having done, but she knew you were having another surgery."

"So, she's jealous because I got to have lots and lots of surgeries?"

"Not because of the surgeries," Josette said, "because of all the time your parents spent with you. Didn't at least one of them fly to the States with you for every one of your surgeries?"

"Yeah," I admitted.

"And wasn't there other stuff?" she asked.

"Like what?"

"I don't know," she replied. "Like therapy or something?"

"I had speech therapy," I said.

She nodded.

"And a couple sets of braces . . ."

"See?" She nodded again. "Your parents spent a *bunch* of time with you while you were growing up. Grace probably felt like they were spending all their time with you instead of her."

"I don't think so."

"Plus," Josette went on, ignoring me, "I know you don't believe this, but you were incredibly cute."

I rolled my eyes at her.

"You *were*, Marco," she insisted. "I can't even imagine the amount of attention you got when you were young, with everyone *oohing* and *ahhhing* over their little *Muñeco* and going on and on about how great your latest surgery went or how well you were enunciating your words . . ."

"And meanwhile," she went on, "there sat little Grace, watching everybody fawn all over you like you were the only cute kid in the room."

"I don't think so," I said again. "I think my parents did a good job of making all of us feel special and loved."

"I'm sure they did," she nodded. "But did your dad ever fly to Boston with Grace and take *her* to a Red Sox game?"

"You know what?" I asked, real anger welling up inside. "I don't feel one bit sorry for Grace just because she didn't get to spend a bunch of 'extra time' with my parents. I gladly would have given up *every single one* of those trips."

"Your mom told me all about why they adopted you," she said, undeterred by my rant.

"So?"

"She said your dad took one look at you on your first day in the orphanage and fell in love with you right then and there. He just had to have you. Your mom said she couldn't have kept the two of you apart if she'd tried."

"So?" I asked again.

"So," she answered, "what about *Grace's* adoption story?"

"What about it?"

"Why did they get her?"

I had a sneaking suspicion that she already knew exactly why Mom and Dad had adopted Grace, but I reluctantly went ahead and told her.

"My dad wanted Amber," I said. "They had to take her little sisters too or they couldn't get her."

She looked at me with a self-satisfied expression on her face, and I felt my anger grow.

"I don't feel sorry for her!" I said again, my voice rising. "My mom and dad love her every bit as much as they love me!"

"But maybe she doesn't realize that–" Josette began before I cut her off.

"If she doesn't realize that, then that's *her* problem," I yelled. "She has had *everything* I've ever had and more."

I had never yelled at Josette before and her eyes widened in surprise, but I was so mad right then that I didn't care.

"She never had to deal with this," I went on, still yelling, shoving my hands in Josette's face. "Things were bad enough without her doing everything she could to make me even more miserable than I already was."

Josette pulled back with a hurt look on her face as I continued on in a bitter voice. "I would trade places with her in a *heartbeat*."

She sat back even further, looking at me, and I knew that I had gone too far . . . that I should apologize. Instead, however, I just looked right back at her until she said, very quietly, "I'd trade places with *you* in a heartbeat," and then she got up off the couch and walked to her bedroom, closing the door behind her.

After Josette left, I sat and stared at the spot where she had been for a moment before turning off the television right in the middle of our show and clearing the coffee table. I put away the meatloaf and the potatoes and I did the dishes all by myself, fully aware that I needed to go apologize to Josette but still feeling too angry to do it. Instead, I went to my room, closed the door, and stretched out on the bed, staring up at the ceiling and thinking about everything she had said. I'd been in there for about ten minutes when I heard the sound of her door opening, followed by a light knock on my own.

"Marco?" she called softly.

By now my anger had been replaced by complete embarrassment at how I'd yelled her and I was quite ready to apologize.

"It's open," I answered, propping myself up on my elbows.

She opened the door slowly and looked in at me.

"May I come in?" she asked tentatively.

I nodded and she stepped into the room.

"I'm sorry," she said quietly.

"Me too," I replied sincerely.

We looked at each other for a moment.

"Can I talk to you for a minute?" she asked.

"About Grace?" I asked, raising my eyebrow.

She shook her head and gave me a little smile.

I sat up even more and patted the end of the bed, inviting her to have a seat. She did.

She looked at me for a moment but then turned to face my closet. She was quiet for a long time.

"When I was sixteen," she finally began in a faraway voice, "Dad bought a house in Perth. I liked it there a lot. After being homeschooled on a yacht for so long I liked being at a big school with lots of classes and lots of kids and different sports and activities and . . ."

"It was exciting," she said, glancing at me briefly. I nodded before she looked away again.

"Stuart was in my biology class," she said, smiling as she remembered. "He was a rugby player and he was really cute and popular and funny and his family had lots of money . . . I didn't think someone like him would ever be interested in me, but for some reason he was. He asked me to go to a party with him and pretty soon we were together all the time."

She hesitated before going on.

"I found out I was pregnant three days before I turned seventeen," she said, pausing to face me again, obviously waiting to see my reaction.

I just gave her another nod.

"Stuart said he wanted to marry me," she went on. "Of course Dad wasn't upset or anything – I think he kind of viewed it as the next great adventure in our lives or whatever – but I made Stuart tell his parents by himself. I was *so* scared how they were going to take it."

"How did they?"

"Surprisingly well," she said, nodding. "Stuart had already been accepted at Sydney and they agreed to pay for a flat for us until he finished school."

I nodded one more time.

"I finished high school just before Jamie was born. Stuart's parents helped us move two months later, and all of a sudden I was a brand-new mom in a strange city, with no family and no friends.

"Stuart was great," she went on. "I was kind of worried that he'd want to be out partying or something, but he really stepped up and did what he needed to do. He played intramurals, but other than that, he did all of his studying at home and he really helped me with Jamie and he played with her all the time and . . ."

Her voice trailed off.

"We were happy," she said. "It was a good life."

I didn't say anything.

"Stuart was the one who wanted to get her baptized," she went on. "He'd grown up going to church and I'd hardly ever been so I didn't really care, but he thought it was something we should do, so I said, 'Okay'. We found a church that we liked and asked them to baptize her, but they said we had to become members first, so we did.

"I liked going there," she said. "I was really lonely in this big new city and the people were really nice and I liked being around them. They invited me to Bible studies and stuff and there was always a nursery so I didn't have to worry about Jamie and it was . . . it was nice."

I shifted my weight on the bed to get more comfortable and then waited for her to continue.

"And I liked church," she said. "I never really knew all that much about God, but I started getting really interested in everything and the more I learned the more I *wanted* to learn, and pretty soon I was reading the Bible every day and praying and . . ."

She shrugged slightly.

"So," she told me, "like I said, life was good. I probably didn't really appreciate it at the time, you know. I wanted to be taking classes too, and I wanted a flat that was closer to the park so I could walk there with Jamie, but overall, things were really good."

She took a big, deep breath, and I looked at her, fairly sure I didn't want hear the rest of this story.

"What happened?" I finally asked when she remained quiet.

She turned away from me and stared at my closet again.

"Jamie was almost four," she said. "Stuart had just graduated and had been accepted into the graduate program here at Melbourne. We'd already come here and picked out a flat and everything, and we were all set to move after the holidays."

She paused for a moment before going on.

"There was this covered dish supper at church and the kids were going to rehearse for the Christmas pageant. Jamie was one of the animals in the manger . . . she was a cow."

Josette smiled, remembering.

"But we forgot that we were supposed to take something for the supper," she said, "so we stopped at the grocery store on our way to church.

"Stuart pulled into a spot and left the car running. It was hot and he told me that he'd wait there while I ran in to get something. Jamie wanted to come with me, but I told her to stay with Daddy. She started crying."

Josette's smile was gone.

"Stuart said, 'Why can't she just go with you?' and I said because it took twice as long when she went in with me because I had to get her in and out of her booster seat and in and out of the shopping trolley and listen to her begging for candy and stuff, and he said he didn't really want to sit there listening to her cry the whole time I was gone."

She was talking more to herself now than to me.

"So I reached into the back and got her out of her booster seat," she said. "I told her that if she stopped crying, she could sit on Daddy's lap and pretend to drive the car. Stuart said if I was already getting her out of her seat anyway, then why couldn't I just take her in with me?"

Her tone was flat now. She seemed completely detached from the story she was telling.

"Both of us acted like it was such a burden to spend time with her . . ."

Her voice faded off and now I knew for sure that I didn't want to hear the rest of this story.

"I ran into the store and got some rolls and cupcakes," she went on, "and then I went back outside. I could see Jamie through the windshield, sitting on Stuart's lap. She saw me coming and waved, and Stuart helped her beep the horn.

"I put the groceries in the back seat, and I held out my arms for her to come to me so that I could put her back into her booster seat. She reached toward me and then . . ."

She paused.

"Someone hit us from behind," she said, her voice emotionless. "It was an elderly man . . . he accidentally stepped on the gas instead of the brakes. He didn't hit us all that hard, but it pushed us into the concrete post that was in front of us and . . ."

She paused again.

"It was the airbag," she finally said. She waited for a long moment before she was able to go on. "One second she was reaching her arms out to me and the next . . ."

She shook her head as if to clear it.

"It was . . . horrific," she said quietly. "Stuart was knocked unconscious – he doesn't remember anything. But I remember everything. No matter what I do, I'll never forget what I saw. I see it in my mind every day."

I wanted to cry, or throw up, or bolt from the room. Instead I managed to say, "I'm so sorry."

She nodded and turned to face me. Her eyes slowly focused as if she was just becoming aware once again that I was there. Her detachment seemed to fade away, and the next time she spoke, her voice had emotion in it again.

"I'm sorry about earlier," she said.

"No," I answered, shaking my head. "It's okay."

"It's just that," she went on, "sometimes I kind of have a hard time feeling sorry for people when . . ."

"When they don't really have anything to complain about?" I suggested.

She gave me something that approached a smile.

"I'm not saying you don't have anything to complain about," she said kindly. "I know that things have been hard for you and–"

"No," I interrupted. "They haven't. Not really. I've got a great life – you're right. I don't have anything to complain about."

She looked at me for a moment as if she were trying to decide if I was just humoring her. I think she finally decided that I wasn't.

"All I was trying to say earlier," she finished, looking at me with something that was even closer to a smile, "is that I can kind of see why Grace might feel a bit resentful. I'm not saying that she has any right to be so mean to you or anything, but I just was hoping that you could try to put yourself in her shoes for a minute."

I nodded.

"And I'm sorry I got so upset earlier," she said.

"I'm sorry I made you upset."

"You didn't."

She gave me a real smile.

"Goodnight, Marco," she said, patting my hand and standing up.

"Goodnight, Josie."

That night I lay awake, stretched out on my bed, for a very long time, thinking about Jamie, a little girl I had never even met, and thinking about how truly precious life is.

And how short.

I wondered if I was really living the life that I wanted to live, and then I decided that no, I wasn't. Not really.

And it was there – lying on my bed that night – that I decided I was going to make some changes.

~ ~ ~

THE NEXT MORNING I got up and cooked chocolate chip pancakes.

"What's the occasion?" Josette asked when she wandered out of her bedroom and saw that the little table in the kitchen that we never used was suddenly set for two.

"Life is short," I answered, pulling out a chair for her.

She gave me a little smile and took a seat.

"I've been thinking a lot about what you told me last night," I said, putting a plate and a glass down in front of her.

"Oh?"

"Yeah." I handed her a fork. "I decided that I'm going to talk to Grace."

"Really?"

"Yeah," I nodded as she poured herself some water.

"What are you going to tell her?"

"That I love her," I said, "and that I'm glad she's my sister."

Josette looked at me skeptically.

"I *am*," I insisted, spearing two pancakes and putting them on her plate.

"Well good," Josette said, giving me another smile as she picked up her glass.

"I've decided something else, too," I went on, sliding the syrup toward her.

"What's that?" she asked, taking a sip of water.

"I'm going to ask Bizzy to marry me."

Josette choked and grabbed for a napkin.

"Because of what I told you last night?" she asked in disbelief, wiping her mouth.

"Life is short," I reminded her.

"It *is* short," she agreed, "but I didn't mean that you had to go and get married."

"But I *want* to get married," I said. "Bizzy is smart and funny and talented and beautiful, and I wanted to ask her to marry me before I even moved here, but I didn't."

Josette looked at me expectantly.

"I don't want to wait anymore," I explained.

"Are you going to move?" she asked, looking mildly alarmed.

"No," I said, shaking my head, "but there's no reason we can't go ahead and get engaged and then get married as soon as we're both through with school. Right?"

"I don't know." Josette shrugged. "She's *your* girlfriend." She picked up the syrup and then added, "But it sounds good to me."

~ ~ ~

GRACE'S WEDDING WAS less than two months away, so I started ring shopping immediately. I went to seven different jewelry stores and looked at hundreds of rings.

Actually I didn't just *look* at them . . . I felt them.

I asked to hold each one. Ring after ring. I held them in my hands and I closed my eyes and I tried to imagine how each one would feel to Bizzy.

More than one jeweler gave me an odd look, but I found that I suddenly didn't really care anymore what people thought of me. Ever since my conversation with Josette, my priorities had changed. Suddenly I knew what was important and what wasn't. I knew what I really wanted in life, and I wasn't afraid to go after it anymore.

I was filled with something that I'd never known before . . . a feeling so foreign to me that I almost couldn't identify it, but after a while I figured out what it was.

Self-confidence.

I found lots of rings that *looked* beautiful, but they didn't particularly *feel* beautiful, and I found some rings that *felt* beautiful but didn't particularly *look* beautiful.

I know that it may not seem important how Bizzy's ring looked since she wasn't even going to be able to see it, but I wanted her to be able to hear in people's voices just how beautiful it was when they saw it, when they told her how beautiful it was and when they told her how much they loved it.

I finally found one with a band of delicate, tapered swirls that trapped a large diamond. There was an interlocking wedding band that went with it, made completely of tiny diamonds and flaring out into swirls all its own.

It was almost perfect.

"What don't you like about it?" Josette asked after I told her all about it that evening.

"It's silver," I said.

"Silver?"

"Yeah," I said. "Silver's cheap. I don't want to get her anything cheap."

"How much was it?"

"I don't know," I admitted. "I quit asking prices after about the four hundredth ring. I just want to find the right one, but I'm figuring if it was silver it was cheap."

"If it was covered in diamonds," she frowned, "I doubt that it was made out of silver. Do you think maybe it was white gold?"

"White gold?" I asked. "What's that?"

The next day Josette met me at the jewelry store during her lunch hour, and I showed her the ring.

"Oh, Marco," she gushed. "It's gorgeous!"

That was the kind of thing I wanted Bizzy to hear when she showed it to people.

"Can I help you two with something?" a voice asked from behind the counter.

"Is that white gold?" Josette asked, pointing down at the ring as the salesman opened door to the display case.

"No ma'am," he said as he reached into the case, pulled it out, and handed it to her. "This is platinum."

"Platinum?" I whispered quietly to Josette as she slipped the set onto her finger and held her hand up in front of her to admire it. "Is that good?"

"Yes, it's good, you idiot!" she said, elbowing me in the ribs. "You're going to *wish* this was silver once you find out how much platinum costs!"

And that was how I found the perfect ring for Bizzy.

~ ~ ~

IN ADDITION TO spending a lot of time thinking about what I wanted in life, I also spent a lot of time during the next few weeks thinking about marriage. I meant everything I'd told Josette about Bizzy – about how she was smart and fun and talented and beautiful. Any guy would be lucky to have Bizzy and I couldn't imagine ever *not* wanting to be with her . . .

But at the same time I thought about all the things that could happen between the two of us over the next sixty or seventy years, and I thought about all the people who uttered the line *'Til death do you part* but who parted way before that . . .

And I wondered.

"Can I ask you a question?" I asked Josette one night after our game show had ended.

"Sure."

"You don't have to tell me if you don't want to."

"What?"

"Why did you and Stuart get divorced?"

"We're not divorced yet," she said. "You have to be separated for a year in Australia before you can get divorced."

"Oh."

"But I can tell you why we're *getting* divorced."

"Okay."

She paused for a moment.

"Losing a child is the worst thing you can go through," she said. "Something like that can either drive you closer together or push you further apart."

I nodded.

"It actually drove us closer together," she said.

I looked at her questioningly.

102

"But it also drives you closer to God," she said, "or further away from Him. I don't think it's possible to stay in the same place once you go through something like that."

I nodded again and waited for her to go on.

"My faith really grew because of what happened with Jamie," she said. "I think I had to rely on Him or I wasn't going to be able to get through. I'm so much closer to Him now than I was before and I don't know how I could have gotten through everything without Him, but . . ."

Her voice trailed off.

"But Stuart's mad at God," she finally said. "Or he doesn't believe in God anymore, or something. I'm not sure. He refuses to talk about it."

"Oh," I said quietly.

"And so me growing closer to God, and him growing farther away . . . it made it so that the two of us couldn't connect on anything anymore. It got to be that the only thing we had in common was the fact that we'd lost Jamie . . . and somehow that wasn't enough."

She paused and lowered her eyes.

"And then he found someone he could connect with," she went on, giving her shoulders a little shrug and looking back up at me. "I came home for lunch one day and found them in bed together. It's not like I surprised him or anything – I came home for lunch all the time. I think he wanted to get caught."

"Oh," I repeated.

"I told him we needed to go to a marriage counselor and he said he didn't want to. He said he wants to be with her. He says he loves her."

"I'm sorry."

"So," she said with another shrug, "I got a hotel room and then I went to the community board at the student union to try to find a place to live and there was nothing there and then you came along with your little piece of paper and now here I am . . . sleeping on your futon every night."

I looked at her sympathetically.

"You and Bizzy are going to be fine," she smiled reassuringly, reaching out to pat my arm. "As long as both of you put God at the center of your marriage and concentrate on what *He* wants, the two of you aren't going to have any problems."

I nodded at her again.

"It's when one of you stops worrying about what God wants," she said, "that the problems start."

~ ~ ~

MY PLAN WAS to propose to Bizzy at either the rehearsal dinner or the reception. When I ran my idea by Josette, however, I didn't get past the part about dropping the ring into Bizzy's champagne glass before she stopped me dead in my tracks.

"No, no, no," she said, shaking her head.

"What?"

"Well, first of all," she said, holding up her thumb. "That's not original at all."

I looked at her.

"Second of all," she extended a finger so that it joined her outstretched thumb, "the last thing you want is for her to *swallow* that ring."

I pursed my lips.

"Third of all," she put another finger out, "the rehearsal dinner and reception are *Grace's* big days. Remember how we talked about the fact that Grace is probably resentful of you for stealing attention away from her all the time? Do you really think she wants everybody gushing over you and Bizzy on *her* big day?"

I was already convinced, but she stuck another finger out anyway and went on.

"Plus Bizzy deserves her own special day, too. Not one that she needs to share with someone else."

"Okay—"

"And," she interrupted, holding all five fingers out now and shaking them for emphasis, "it needs to be done in *private* . . . just the two of you. Something *romantic*."

"Okay," I agreed again, nodding, and I was glad when she didn't start in with the fingers on her other hand.

BEFORE THE WEDDING, Grace was playing the role of Bridezilla as if she'd invented it. She was immediately mad at me when I arrived in California because I rented a BMW convertible for the week and she insisted that I was trying to steal her thunder. (Imagine how ticked she would have been if I'd proposed to Bizzy in front of all of her wedding guests or something like I had originally planned.)

Oh, Josie, you are a wise woman.

Of course I hadn't rented the car to make Grace mad – I hadn't even considered the fact that it might make her mad. I just wanted Bizzy to feel the rush of the wind in her hair, hear the scream of the engine, enjoy the smell and feel of the leather seats.

Yeah. That's why.

Anyway, Bizzy and I were both going to be in Monterey for six days, and when I found her I wrapped my arms around her and I kissed her and then I held her tight. It had been almost a year since I'd seen her and that had been far too long. I couldn't wait until Grace's wedding was over so that the two of us could start planning ours.

It's easier to *imagine* having a heartfelt moment with someone than it is to actually *have* a heartfelt moment . . . especially when that someone (who should be concentrating on something like, oh, say . . . getting married) still takes time to go out of her way to embarrass you in front of everybody. Especially when that someone still insists on tormenting you even though you haven't done anything to them and even though you're *trying* to be nice to them. Especially when that someone is Grace.

By the time the rehearsal dinner was over on Friday night I had pretty much given up on the idea of talking to Grace. That night, however, I thought once again about Jamie and I thought about how short life was and I thought about how I would really feel if something were to ever happen to Grace . . .

And so I made up my mind – one more time – that I was going to try to talk to her.

The next day I waited until just before Dad was set to walk her down the aisle. When I stuck my head in the parlor and asked Grace to step out into the hall to talk to me for a minute, she started shrieking at me that I was supposed to be sitting down already. With my newfound confidence, however, I held my ground and insisted that she come out and talk to me. Reluctantly she joined me in the hall, standing before me, and looking not unpretty, in a glittery white gown.

"What?" she demanded, stomping her foot.

"I just want to tell you that I love you," I said.

She eyed me suspiciously and I put my hands on her arms.

I looked steadily into her eyes.

"I know it was hard on you to grow up with me as your brother," I began carefully. "Mom and Dad always had to do so much to take care of me and I'm sure it must have felt to you like I was always getting all the attention all the time."

She didn't say anything, but her face softened.

"And I'm sorry," I went on. "I mean, obviously I couldn't help it or anything, but I'm sorry that they had to spend so much time with me."

She pursed her lips and swallowed hard.

"And I just wanted to say that I'm really glad you're my sister," I said, leaning forward and giving her a kiss on the cheek. "And I love you, okay?"

She nodded at me as I pulled away from her and I saw tears in her eyes.

"Now go get married," I said, and I steered her back toward the parlor.

Bizzy and I were both going to be in California for three more days, and we were already planning to spend the entire day after the wedding with one another. I dropped her off at her room the evening of the wedding, kissing her lips gently and telling her to be sure to wear her bathing suit under her clothes the next day.

"Where are we going?" she wanted to know.

"Big Sur," I answered.

Big Sur is located south of Monterey and we took Highway 1, south past Carmel. I let Bizzy know when we got to the beginning of Bixby Bridge and I told her when we had reached the end, because I wanted her to know how long it was and I wanted her to know how high up we were and I wanted her to know that she was on one of the most famous bridges in the world.

I wished that she could see it . . . I wished that she could see everything that I saw as we drove along the beautiful Pacific coastline. But at least she had the wind in her hair and the scream of the engine and the smell and the feel of the leather seats.

Not too long after the bridge, I found the road I was looking for and took a sharp right turn, continuing on until we reached a parking area. After that, we grabbed our stuff and walked down the trail to the beach, dropping our things onto the sand and stripping down to our suits.

"Come on," I said after I'd taken her hand and led her to the waterline. "We're going to look for jade."

"Jade?"

"Yeah," I said. "You're supposed to be able to find it on most of the beaches around here."

Josette had helped me do a lot of research to find this particular beach. There were other places where jade was apparently easier to find, but they were all too rocky or too hard for a blind person to get to or walk on, or too likely to have giant waves that could sweep naïve tourists like me and Bizzy out to sea.

Plus, it didn't really matter if we found jade or not. The plan was to let her dig around for a little while searching for jade, and then I would put the ring down on the sand and wait for her to discover it. I couldn't wait to watch her face light up as she realized what it was that she was holding.

"Okay," Bizzy said with a smile, and even though she couldn't see me, I smiled back.

Bizzy was always ready for anything.

~ ~ ~

FOUR DAYS LATER I opened the front door to my little house and found Josette lying on the couch, reading a book. She sat up to make room for me as soon as she saw me, her mouth stretching into a huge grin.

"Well?" she asked excitedly, reaching out and hitting my arm lightly as I plopped down next to her. "How'd it go?"

"It was a very nice wedding," I answered.

"Not *that*, you idiot! Did Bizzy like the ring?"

"You mean this ring?" I asked and I took it out of my jacket pocket and held it up. Apparently Bizzy hadn't been as "ready for anything" as I'd thought.

Josette's eyes widened and her face fell.

"What happened?" she asked softly, her mouth now slightly open in shock.

"She didn't think we needed to be engaged right now," I said, shrugging slightly.

"Why not?" Josette asked, her mouth still open in disbelief.

"Because she wants to be in Venezuela by this time next year and she doesn't know exactly how long she'll be there or whatever and she doesn't want to get engaged when everything's so up in the air."

"Oh," Josette said. "So, maybe later?"

"No," I said, shaking my head. "It's over."

"Why?" she asked, her eyes growing wide again.

"Because we broke up."

"You broke up?" she cried, her eyes managing to widen even more, and I nodded. *"Why?"*

My newfound self-confidence had kicked into full swing once I'd realized that Bizzy wasn't going to accept the ring I'd bought her. I hadn't exactly given her an ultimatum ... but almost.

110

I don't think Bizzy was too impressed with the new me. Bizzy wasn't exactly lacking in self-confidence herself, and she certainly wasn't going to let herself be pushed into something she wasn't ready for.

"She said we needed some time to 'think'," I explained, doing my best to make little quote marks in the air.

"And what exactly does that mean?" she asked.

"It means it's over."

She eyed me dubiously.

"It is," I insisted.

Josette continued to look at me for a long moment.

"I'm really sorry," she finally said softly.

"It's okay," I shrugged. "I guess it just wasn't meant to be."

She looked at me now, obviously surprised that I wasn't more distraught. I had, after all, been dating Bizzy for almost nine years, and by all rights, breaking up with her should have left me devastated.

It didn't though. And I thought I knew why.

My new attitude, combined with the fact that I'd already had four days to get used to it, was part of the reason I wasn't more upset.

I think the main reason, though, was because of my faith.

My faith had always been important to me. I had walked forward at a youth retreat when I was fourteen and publicly accepted Christ as my personal savior. I memorized Scripture. I read my Bible. I witnessed to people. I prayed (especially when I needed something). So, like I said, my faith was important to me.

Secretly, however, I think I had always worried that my faith wouldn't be strong enough to see me through a really difficult time. That's why I was so pleased now to find out that I was doing just fine. I had a certainty in my heart that God loved me, and I knew that He had a plan for me. I knew that He wasn't going to let me go through something unless He was ultimately going to work it for good.

My faith . . . *that's* why I was doing so well.

"I'm really sorry," Josette said again.

"Thanks," I sighed, sinking back into the couch.

We sat quietly for a moment.

"On the bright side," I said, holding the ring up again, "I can return this at *any* time for full store credit."

I glanced at her and she gave me a little smile.

"I guess my mom and sisters are going to be getting jewelry for Christmas this year," I said, sighing again.

She looked at me for a moment.

"My birthstone's sapphire," she said, and I felt my eyes narrow.

"Well, you know," she said, shrugging innocently. "Just in case you were wondering."

I glared at her and she smiled again, sitting forward on the couch.

"I'm going to get you something that'll make you feel better," she said, patting me on the knee.

"Not Vegemite."

"No," she agreed, standing up and heading toward the kitchen. "Ice cream."

That actually didn't sound too bad. I watched as she opened the freezer and took out a carton and then reached into the fridge to retrieve the chocolate syrup. She pried open the lid to the ice cream and began dumping syrup straight into the container.

"Umm, don't you want to put that in a bowl first?" I asked.

"Oh, no," she said adamantly, shaking her head as she continued to add more chocolate. "You have to eat it straight out of the container when you've got a broken heart."

"You do?"

"Yes," she nodded, giving the syrup bottle a final squeeze. "And you've gotta watch a chick flick while you're eating it."

"A chick flick?" I asked, raising an eyebrow at her skeptically.

"Or *Chances Are*," she smiled, reaching into the drawer for a spoon. "I recorded it again the whole time you were gone."

I smiled back at her as she returned to the living room and handed me the container.

"Thank you," I said, taking it from her. "I feel better already."

"You're welcome."

I set the ring down on the coffee table in front of us and took a bite of ice cream.

"Don't forget," Josette said, picking up the remote and glancing at the ring before she turned on the TV. "Sapphires."

~ ~ ~

OF COURSE WHEN I said that I felt God had something better in mind, I pretty much figured He had some*one* better in mind.

I do fully realize that not everyone is going to find that "someone special" to love, and I know that it's not God's plan for everyone to get married, but – just like I had when I was younger – I somehow still had a certainty in my heart that there was someone out there for me. I'm not exactly sure *how* I knew this, but I did. The only thing I didn't know was how I was supposed to go about finding her.

The number of women I knew in Australia was relatively small: there was Lisa (the lady in accounting who ran all of our material orders), Kerilee, Sandra, Kate and Noelle (the girls who worked in my research lab), Angelique (the girl who worked in the science research library), and Robin (the lady I had gotten to know a bit who worked at the cafeteria).

I was confident that none of these women were my "someone special."

Lisa was about sixty years old, and Robin was probably closer to seventy. Call me prejudiced, but I crossed them off my mental list while I was making it.

Kerilee and Angelique were both married.

Noelle was pregnant.

Kate was gay.

Sandra was mean.

My pool of prospective new girlfriends was not exactly overflowing.

You can do anything you put your mind to, Marco . . .

For my entire life, my parents had told me this, and I had always believed them. I'd graduated summa cum laude from one of the top schools in the United States. I was going to graduate school at one of the top universities in the world, and I was working with world-renowned researchers at one of the premier institutes in my field. I could play sports and throw darts and write my name and type reports and cut my food and button my shirts.

I could do anything . . .

But find somebody to love?

I knew that God could put someone in my life any time He wanted . . . but what if He didn't decide to miraculously drop some woman on my doorstep? What if He expected me to actually get out there and make it happen myself?

How was I supposed to do that?

Such a task would have been easy for someone like my brother. Dorito could have a cleft palate, missing fingers, and a horn growing out of the middle of his forehead, but he still would have been able to make friends wherever he went.

But I wasn't like Dorito – not by a long shot.

The *feísimo* factor had undoubtedly contributed to my reserved nature, but I was fairly certain that being somewhat shy and reserved was also just a natural part of who I was.

But could I *do* something about that? Could I change something like that about myself?

You can do anything you put your mind to, Marco . . .

Maybe.

~ ~ ~

TWO WEEKS LATER Josette and I were both slumped
back on the couch, waiting for the commercials to end before
the final round on *Chances Are.*

"So I wanted to let you know that I'm not going to church
with you Sunday," I mentioned, as casually as I could.

"How come?" she asked, unconcerned.

"I, um," I hesitated. "I've decided that I'm going to try
some different churches."

"You're what?" she asked, sitting up and looking at me,
definitely concerned now. "Why?"

"You know," I said, shrugging and still going for casual. "I
just think I'm kind of looking for something different."

"What's wrong with Hope Springs?"

"Nothing's wrong with it," I said. "I just want to go
somewhere else."

"*Why?*"

"I just do."

"Marco," she said seriously, "what's going on?"

"Nothing's going on," I insisted. "This really isn't a big
deal."

"Well it's a big deal to me!"

"Why?"

"Because I like going to church with you!"

"Well I like going to church with you, too, but . . ."

"But what?"

I looked at her and sighed. Sometimes I *really* wished I
could lie.

"Look, I just . . ." I sighed again. "I just want to meet some
new people."

"New people," she repeated flatly.

I nodded.

"What's wrong with the people at Hope Springs?"

116

"There's nothing wrong with them," I admitted, shaking my head, "but . . ."

"But what?" she asked, staring at me expectantly.

I looked back at her. This was *so* embarrassing.

"Bizzy's out of the picture now," I finally forced myself to answer. "And I just think that if there's somebody else out there for me, maybe I have to go *find* her. You know what I mean?"

"Oh," she said slowly.

"So," I went on, "I thought that going to a new church might be a good place to start."

"Are you going to go to one of those big mega-churches that has a singles group or something?"

"I don't think so," I said, shaking my head. "I don't know exactly what I'm going to do, but I just think I need to get out there a bit and see what happens . . . you know? Get out of my comfort zone?"

"Oh," she said again.

"So," I said, "I just wanted to let you know."

"Right," she said, and she nodded, seemingly in agreement.

A few hours later though, after we'd both said goodnight to each other and gone to bed, Josette knocked on my door.

"Come in," I said, reaching for the light next to my bed.

She opened the door as I turned it on.

"Can I talk to you for a minute?" she asked.

"Sure," I answered. I drew my feet up so that she could sit down on the end of my bed.

The last time she'd come into my room and sat down on my bed to talk to me like that she'd shaken up my entire world . . .

She was about to do it again.

"I had an idea," she said.

"What's that?"

"Why don't we go out?"

"Now? Where?"

"No," she said impatiently. "I mean like on a date."

"What?"

"I was thinking that you and I could go out on a date."

I felt my eyes widen in surprise.

"Why?"

"Well, because you just said that you wanted to start dating someone."

"Well, yeah," I sputtered, "but I didn't mean *you*."

Wow . . . did that ever come out wrong.

"That came out wrong," I said hastily.

"Forget it," she said, starting to stand up.

"No, wait." I reached forward to grab her arm. "You don't understand."

"Understand what?"

"You're . . . you're like my best friend here, Josie. Heck, you're my *only* friend."

She looked at me, waiting for me to go on.

"And if we try to date and it doesn't work out . . ." I let go of her arm, looking at her in hopes that she would understand. "Do we really want to take a chance on messing that up?"

"Probably not," she agreed. "I guess it was a stupid idea."

"No," I said. "It wasn't a stupid idea, but . . ."

"Forget I said anything." She began to stand up again.

"I mean, it's nice of you to ask and everything," I said, not stopping her this time.

"Don't worry about it," she said, heading for the door. "Good night."

And she left.

So.

Back to my mental list.

Of course Josette had been on it . . . for like *two* seconds.

If I'd thought that things might actually work out between me and Josette I might have actually considered taking her up on her offer (even though she really *was* the best friend I had right then and even though I really *didn't* want to mess that up).

I would have been willing to risk losing that friendship if I'd honestly thought there was a chance for the two of us . . . but there was no chance.

Just as I still believed that there was someone out there for me, I also still believed that that "someone" would belong on the Island of Misfit Toys like I did. I was certain that there was going to be something majorly wrong with whoever I wound up with . . .

And to put it bluntly, there was nothing wrong with Josette.

Josette was way out of my league. She belonged on the *antipode* of the Island of Misfit Toys . . . clear on the other side of the world. You can't live with a woman for almost a year and not notice something like that . . . whether or not they're attractive.

And Josette most definitely was.

Her eyes, for example. I had actually noticed them the moment I met her in the student union that first day, so long ago. They were a dark, charcoal gray and they were framed by incredibly thick, black lashes and they were beautiful . . . and I had immediately felt guilty for even noticing them.

It wasn't just her eyes, though.

Everything about Josette was attractive: the soft curve of her lips, the gentle arch of her perfectly sculpted eyebrows, her high cheekbones and long, straight dark hair, the flawless tone of her bronzed skin, her delicate fingers, her . . .

No. There was absolutely nothing wrong with Josette.

Except for maybe the fact that she hardly ever laughed.

And except for the reason behind the fact that she hardly every laughed . . .

I scrambled out of bed and crossed the small hallway, knocking on Josette's door.

"Come in?"

"Uhhh, hi," I said, opening her door. She was sitting up in bed with a book in front of her.

"Hi . . ." She raised a perfectly sculpted eyebrow at me.

"So, uhh." I ran my hand nervously through my hair. "I was thinking about what you said and I changed my mind. I think we should definitely go out."

"I thought you didn't want to take a chance on messing up our friendship."

"I don't," I admitted, "but we can be mature, right? We'll just make up our minds that if it doesn't work out we'll pretend like it never happened and go back to being friends."

"We don't have to go out, Marco," she said, shaking her head. "It's not really that big of a deal."

"But I *want* to go out with you," I insisted. "You just caught me off guard."

"Are you sure?"

"Yeah," I said. "I'm sure."

"And no matter what happens we'll still be friends?"

"Absolutely."

"Okay," she finally agreed.

It was Thursday.

"Tomorrow night?" I suggested.

"Okay," she said again.

"Great," I replied. "It's a date."

I got home the next evening about half of an hour before Josette did. Once she came through the door, she dropped her purse onto the couch, went into the bathroom for a minute, and then reemerged, putting her purse back over her shoulder and asking me if I was ready to go.

"You're ready already?" I asked.

"Uh-huh."

"You're, uh, you're not going to change or anything?"

"Change?"

"Yeah."

"Into what?"

"I dunno," I shrugged. "I just thought you might want to put on something different or do something different with your hair or . . . something."

"What's wrong with the way I look right now?"

"Nothing," I admitted, "but you're wearing the same thing you wore to work and I just thought that you might want to, uh, I don't know . . . do something special."

"Special?"

"You know," I explained. "Freshen up your makeup or something."

"I'm not *wearing* any makeup."

"Well, I thought maybe you'd want to put some on or something."

She raised that eyebrow at me again.

"You want me to put on makeup?"

"I mean . . . only if you want to."

She stared at me for a moment and then dropped her purse back onto the couch, turning on her heel and returning to the bathroom.

She wasn't gone long, but when she came back out she had the brightest, reddest lipstick I'd ever seen in my entire life smeared all over her lips.

And I mean *smeared*. All over. She'd gone out of her way to not keep it on her lips.

"Happy now?" she asked, picking her purse up again.

I pressed my own lips together and nodded silently, and then we left the house without another word.

We were about halfway to the restaurant before I finally dared to take my eyes off the road to glance at Josette. She had crossed her arms as soon as we got into the car, and they were still crossed.

"You aren't really going to go into the restaurant like that, are you?" I finally asked.

"So now you want me to take it off?" she asked, glaring at me. "I thought you wanted me to do something *special*."

"Josette . . ."

"Don't 'Josette' me," she snapped, taking a tissue out of her purse and wiping her mouth. "I don't know how come you can go out on a date looking the *exact same way* you did all day, but I have to do something special."

"You don't," I insisted. "I was just surprised, that's all. I just thought you'd want to do something different."

"*You* didn't do anything different," she pointed out.

"What am I supposed to do?" I protested. "I'm a guy! What are guys supposed to do that's special?"

She crossed her arms again and looked out the window.

"Look, Josette," I said. "I'm sorry, okay?"

"Whatever," she muttered.

"This is why we shouldn't be going out," I muttered right back.

"What?"

"I *said*," I answered, my voice getting louder, "'This is why we shouldn't be going out.'"

She looked at me.

"You're all mad at me now," I explained, shaking my head. "I knew this was a bad idea."

She sighed and I saw her body relax a bit.

"I'm not mad at you," she said as we pulled into the parking lot.

"Yes, you are," I argued, "and if you stay mad at me then I'm not going to have anyone to watch TV with or eat with . . ."

"Or anyone to do your dishes . . ."

I glanced at her again and she cocked that eyebrow at me.

"Look," I said, pulling into a spot. "I said I was sorry. Can we . . . can we just start over or something?"

I put the car in park and looked at her again. She nodded at me.

"I'm sorry, too," she said.

I breathed a little sigh of relief, and when we headed into the restaurant, I still had hope that the two of us were at least going to be able to salvage our friendship.

Josette was apparently hoping the same thing because she was overly polite from that point on. It was nice not to argue with her anymore, but our usual friendly banter was gone, replaced by forced conversations and strained silences. When Josette suggested that we see a movie after dinner, I jumped at the opportunity to not have to talk to her for two hours.

The movie was quite possibly the worst I'd ever seen in my life. It was actually painful to watch, managing somehow to be both juvenile and raunchy at the same time, and adding a whole new level of awkwardness to our date. We left the movie in silence, remaining quiet for most of the ride home, only speaking to each other long enough to agree how horrible it had been. We arrived home, and after that, things got *really* awkward.

"Well," Josette said once I'd unlocked the door and the two of us were standing in the living room. "Thank you for dinner."

"Thank you," I said. "I had a nice time."

I saw a small smile cross her lips.

"You're still a terrible liar," she said, and I gave her a little smile of my own. Then we looked at each other and I wondered what we were supposed to do next.

Hug? Kiss? Shake hands?

Josette made the decision.

"Well goodnight," she said, reaching out and giving me three little pats on the arm. "I'm going to turn in. I'm really tired."

I decided that she was a pretty bad liar herself.

I went into my bedroom, letting her have the bathroom first, and I checked my messages. I returned one of them, and – after I heard her bedroom door close – I went into the bathroom and brushed my teeth. Once I was ready for bed, I tried to read for a few minutes, but before long I gave up and stared at the ceiling . . . just like I had the night before.

And I started thinking . . . just like I had the night before.

And after a bit of that, I scrambled out of bed and knocked on Josette's door . . . just like I had the night before.

"Come in."

I opened the door and found her sitting up in bed again, apparently having better luck reading than I'd had. She lowered her book and looked at me expectantly.

"I want to try again," I told her.

"What?"

"I think we should go out again. Tomorrow night."

Her face darkened.

"We don't need to do that, Marco," she said, shaking her head. "Everything's fine right now. I think we'd better quit while we're ahead."

"No," I said adamantly, shaking my head too. "I can do better. I want to try again."

"You don't have to 'do better'," she argued. "You didn't do anything wrong. We gave it a shot and it didn't work out and–"

"I want to try again," I interrupted.

She looked at me for a moment and then asked very quietly, "Why?"

"I just do," I insisted. "Please? Give me one more chance. Go out with me again tomorrow night . . . please?"

She looked at me very carefully and finally nodded.

"Great," I said. "I'll pick you up at six."

That made her laugh.

"Okay," she agreed. "I'll see you at six."

~ ~ ~

THE NEXT MORNING I waited until I knew Josette was in the kitchen before I left my bedroom, dragging a small suitcase behind me. I had a smaller, overnight bag that I could have used instead, but a suitcase seemed more dramatic.

"I'll see you tonight at six," I said, standing before the front door.

"Where are you going?" she asked, turning away from the coffeepot and looking at me in surprise.

"I'm going to a hotel," I announced.

"A *hotel*?"

"Yep."

"Why?"

"Because," I said. "If we're going on a date I should pick you up and drop you off. I want it to be special."

"So you're staying at a *hotel*," she repeated slowly.

"Yes."

"To make it special."

"Yes."

"Marco," she said, tipping her head at me disapprovingly. "You don't have to do that."

"I want to."

She looked at me for a moment.

"Well what am I supposed to do?" she asked.

"Do whatever you want," I shrugged. "Enjoy your day and don't worry about anything. I've got everything taken care of."

She stared at me for another moment.

"Any other questions?" I asked when she didn't say anything further.

"I guess not," she replied uncertainly.

"Good," I smiled, nodding as I went out the front door. Then I reminded her, "I'll pick you up at six."

By the time I returned that evening, my brand-new blazer was already damp from all the times I'd wiped it with my sweaty palms and I was really glad that I had gone with something dark.

I rang my doorbell and waited anxiously for Josette to answer.

Once she opened the door, I held my hands out to my side and looked at her expectantly. She gasped when she saw me, bringing both hands up to cover her gaping mouth. She continued staring at me, wide-eyed, while I slowly turned around, hands still out to my side, making a complete circle. Once I'd gone all the way around, I stood motionless in front of her, waiting nervously for her to say something.

But she didn't say anything . . . she didn't even move. She just continued to stand there with her eyes wide and her hands clamped over her mouth.

"Well?" I finally dared to ask. "How do I look?"

I had never before in my life asked anybody that question.

She pulled her hands down slowly from her mouth.

"You shaved your moustache off," she whispered, putting her hands over her heart.

I nodded and swallowed hard.

She continued to stare at me, her mouth still hanging open, her hands still against her chest.

"I was trying to do something special," I managed after a bit. "What do you think?"

"You look so young," she said in a whisper. "I can't believe what a baby face you have."

"No," I disagreed seriously, shaking my head. "My baby face didn't look anything like this."

That evening there was no uncomfortable silence . . . no strained conversation . . . no awkward movie. There was just talking and laughing and smiling and stopping for ice cream on the way home.

126

When we got back to the house I opened Josette's car door for her and gave her my arm to hold as we walked up the sidewalk to the porch. My palms had stopped being sweaty a long time ago. Once we reached the top of the stairs, Josette asked me if I was going to come in, but I shook my head.

"No," I said, "but I'd like to sit out here with you for a while."

She looked at me for a quick moment and then agreed.

"Okay," she said. "Let me just go in and get a cardigan."

"Do you want my jacket?" I offered, reaching to take it off.

"No," she said, shaking her head. "I'll be right back.

I nodded and she disappeared into the house. I waited for her on the top step of the porch since neither one of my chairs sat too good since that day I'd thrown them.

Josette came out a minute later and sat down next to me, holding a blanket instead of a cardigan.

"Would you like to share?" she asked, holding it up. She opened it behind my back and I nodded.

I reached to help her put the blanket around us both and then, after just a brief moment of hesitation, I put my arm around her. She leaned toward me as I did, resting her head against my shoulder, and we sat like that together, not talking, for several long minutes.

Eventually I broke the silence, quietly asking her, "What are you thinking right now?"

There was a slight pause.

"That I like being here like this with you," she answered. Then she asked softly, "What are *you* thinking?"

I paused too, but only for a second.

"That I really want this to work."

She pulled away from me so that I could see her face, and her lips came together in a little smile. She looked at me with such warmth in her eyes that – for a moment – I actually thought she was going to kiss me.

She didn't though. Instead, she gave her head a slight shake and whispered, "I can't believe you shaved your moustache off."

I looked back at her. It was getting hard to see in the fading light, but I knew that she had been able to see plenty earlier. I also knew that she'd tell me the truth.

"Can you see it?" I asked.

She reached up, gently touching my scar, lightly tracing a finger where my moustache had been only hours earlier. I closed my eyes at her touch.

"Yes," I heard her whisper, and I swallowed hard.

"It's part of who you are," she went on, still running her fingernail across my lip. "I love it."

I opened my eyes and looked down at her as she brought her hand to the side of my face and then to my neck, where she let it rest.

Now I was *sure* she was going to kiss me, so I closed my eyes again . . .

But she didn't kiss me . . .

Not exactly . . .

She kissed my scar.

Goosebumps covered my entire body at the feel of her lips on my skin and I drew in a sharp, jagged breath over the pounding of my heart. When she pulled away, I opened my eyes again and found her looking at me intently.

"Now what are you thinking?" she asked in a quiet voice.

I looked back at her for a moment before I was able to find my own voice.

"That I really, *really* want this to work," I said.

Another little smile formed on her lips. I reached to the corner of her mouth, and when my hand touched her face, she closed her eyes.

I traced my thumb across her lips and then I stroked my hand along her cheek. With her eyes still closed, she slowly reached her hand up and covered mine.

She held my hand against her face for a moment. Then she turned her face so that once again her lips were touching my hand.

Then she kissed it, too.

After she kissed my hand, Josette pressed it against her cheek again and I marveled at the sight of it against her skin.

It was the first time in my life I had ever liked the way my hand looked.

She opened her eyes and stared at me intently once more. I looked back at her now, my heart beating so hard I could barely breathe. This time, when she closed her eyes again, I leaned toward her and brought my lips to hers, covering her mouth with mine.

It was a kiss unlike any I'd ever had.

Josette didn't just let me kiss her, she kissed me back.

Her lips were warm and soft and as they parted beneath mine she pressed her body against me, wrapping an arm around my waist and pulling me even closer. I was sure that I could feel her heart, pounding as wildly as mine, until finally – desperate for air – we pulled slightly apart from one another. I couldn't do anything after that except rest my forehead against hers, trying to catch my breath.

We both sat there like that, gasping for air, until I finally managed to say, "Wow."

"Yeah," she agreed with a little laugh. "Wow."

And then we kissed again.

~ ~ ~

THE NEXT MORNING I got to Sunday School later than I meant to. I scanned the room and didn't see Josette yet, but I quickly spotted two seats on the opposite side of the circle and I headed that way. I put my Bible down in one chair to save it for Josette, but before I could sit in the other one, someone said good morning to me and started making small talk. By the time they were finished, the empty chair had been taken by someone else, who now also greeted me and also wanted to make small talk. Unsure of how to find another place to sit without being rude, I picked up my Bible and sat down, trying to converse politely while at the same time keeping an eye on the door.

When Josette came in I looked straight at her so that I could mouth "Sorry" to her for not having saved her a chair, but she wouldn't make eye contact. Instead, she sat down across the circle from me and greeted the person sitting next to her. I kept staring at her, but she wouldn't look back. Finally I realized that she was purposefully *not* looking my way.

My heart sank.

Was she already sorry that we'd gone out? Embarrassed at the thought of people finding out we had?

It was amazing how quickly all those feelings of insecurity that had plagued me while I'd been dating Bizzy came flooding back to me now.

I actually felt sick to my stomach.

Why? Why does this always happen?

But then another thought came to me just as quickly. What if *Josette* was the one who was worried about how *I* felt?

I continued thinking about this possibility and, after a moment, I pulled out my phone and sent Josette a text: *You look beautiful.*

I watched as she reached into her purse and pulled out her phone. After she read it, she looked up at me for the first time since she'd entered the room and gave me a smile – and every ounce of insecurity I'd had immediately washed away.

She turned back to her phone and answered, *Thank you*, and then she looked back up, still smiling.

I responded, *Wanna go somewhere and make out?*

She glanced down at her phone and looked back at me, her mouth dropping open in disbelief. She started punching away at her phone.

Marco! We're in church!

I know, I answered. *I bet we could find a storage closet somewhere.*

She covered her mouth with one hand, trying unsuccessfully to hide a laugh. *We're in CHURCH!*

She watched me as I read that message, and when I finished I looked back at her and gave her my best "You can't blame a guy for trying" shrug.

She smiled at me again and I sent her one final text: *Will you go on a picnic with me for lunch?*

I'd love to, she texted, and she smiled at me once again.

I smiled back at her, and then we opened our Bibles to get ready for our lesson.

A major tourist attraction in Melbourne was Fitzroy Gardens. There were fountains and sculptures and trees and flowers and even a little lake. There was a preserved trunk called the Scarred Tree that had a scar on it from where Aboriginal people had removed bark to make something, and another one called the Fairies Tree that some famous artist had carved a bunch of gnomes and fairies and stuff in. I had never been there before but had always meant to go, and I figured that today would be a good day to try it out.

As we got closer, however, Josette got quieter and quieter, and when we finally arrived and I started looking for a parking spot, she turned to me and put her hand on my arm.

"I don't want to go here," she said. I glanced at her, surprised by the distressed look on her face. I stopped the car, not caring about the traffic behind me.

"Why?"

"I just don't want to," she said quietly. "Please?"

Impatient drivers began pulling out to go around me.

"Sure," I said, and I moved forward until I found a place to turn around.

"I'm sorry," Josette said after we were back on the main road, headed away from the gardens.

"It's okay," I assured her.

There was a moment of silence before she spoke again.

"We went there," she said softly. "When we came to look at flats and stuff . . . we took Jamie there."

"Oh," I said. "I'm sorry."

"No," she replied, putting her hand on my arm again and shaking her head. "You didn't know. I'm the one who's sorry . . . I'm ruining all your plans."

"It's no problem."

"You went to so much trouble," she said miserably.

"I picked up a bucket of chicken, Josie," I said, tipping my head at her. "It's not that much trouble."

"No," she said. "I mean planning where we should go and everything."

"It's not a big deal," I assured her. "You can have a picnic anywhere."

She looked at me skeptically.

"You can," I said. "As long as you've got a place to sit and some sunshine, you can have a picnic."

She gave me another doubtful look so I drove two blocks farther and turned into a deserted parking lot, pulling my car into a spot.

"What are you doing?" she asked when I turned off the ignition.

"Proving that you can have a picnic anywhere."

"At a *bank*?"

"Uh-huh," I said. "See that grass?"

She nodded.

"See that sun?"

She nodded again.

"Looks like an excellent picnic spot to me." I shrugged and opened my door.

Josette didn't argue when I asked her to carry our drinks. I set the chicken down and spread a blanket on the grass, and by the time we had lowered ourselves onto it, she was almost smiling.

"I'm sorry I ruined everything," she said, nodding back in the direction of Fitzroy Gardens.

"You didn't ruin anything," I said, shaking my head. I leaned forward and kissed her lips gently, bringing my hands to the sides of her face.

When I was finished, I pulled back and looked at her.

"If anyone needs to apologize," I said, "it's me."

"You didn't know," she said.

"No," I said, shaking my head. "Not about that."

"About what then?"

"About yesterday."

"Yesterday?"

I nodded.

"What about yesterday?"

"I tried really hard to make things special," I began.

"You did," she said. "It was wonderful."

"But you worked really hard too," I said. "Didn't you?"

She tipped her head at me curiously and didn't say anything.

"But I didn't even mention it," I went on.

"What do you mean?" she asked.

"That was a new dress you were wearing, wasn't it?"

"I borrowed it from Brenda," she explained.

"Well, you looked beautiful in it," I told her, and she smiled at me appreciatively.

"And your hair," I went on. "It was all in a . . ."

"French braid?" she suggested.

"Yeah," I agreed. "A French braid. That looked beautiful, too."

"Brenda," she said again.

"Did you use some of Brenda's perfume?" I asked.

She nodded. I reached out and took her hand.

"And did she do your nails, too?" I asked.

She nodded again and smiled sheepishly.

"Did you and Brenda have an extreme makeover day or something?" I asked as a car pulled up to the ATM.

Josette giggled and nodded a third time.

"So that explains why your makeup looked so good," I mused, rubbing my chin thoughtfully.

"Hey!" she protested, swatting me.

"I've seen how you put on makeup," I reminded her, catching her arm and pulling her toward me. She laughed again.

"You don't need a makeover at all," I said quietly, "but I wanted to let you know that I noticed everything you did yesterday and I should have said something."

"It's okay," she assured me.

"No, it's not," I argued. "A good boyfriend would have said something."

"Are you my boyfriend?"

"Well, I want to be," I said, and she smiled. I smiled back, but then I turned serious, leaning closer to her and whispering, "I want to be a good boyfriend to you."

"You already are," she whispered back, and she put her hand on the back of my neck and pulled me toward her for a kiss.

The car at the ATM blew its horn.

"What's *their* problem?" I asked, pulling away from her and glancing toward the car. "Haven't they ever seen somebody having a picnic before?"

Josette laughed and drew me in for another kiss.

~ ~ ~

THAT NIGHT, BACK in my own bed, I lay quietly, staring up at the ceiling once again and thinking about everything that had happened since we'd sat on the front porch the evening before. I lay there and thought for a long, long time until finally I forced myself to get out of bed and go into the hallway. I knocked lightly on Josette's door.

"Come in," she said, and I saw the light come on underneath the door.

"Sorry," I said. "Were you asleep yet?"

"Not hardly," she answered, smiling at me. She sat up, drawing her knees to her chest so that I could sit down on the end of her futon, which I did.

I looked at her for a long while. Her hair was falling down around her face and spilling onto the t-shirt she was wearing. I reached up to brush a strand of it from her cheek.

"We need to talk about something," I said, tucking the hair behind her ear.

"What?"

I held her gaze for another moment and then leaned forward, pulling her toward me and lightly touching my lips to hers.

She kissed me back gently at first, but soon there was nothing light or gentle about what we were doing, and any desire I'd had to talk was quickly replaced by something else. After a moment, however, I somehow managed to stop, and I pulled away from her, amazed at how quickly she could leave me breathless. I rested my forehead against hers as I had the night before, eyes closed, one hand wrapped in her hair, the other around her waist.

"One of us has to move out," I finally said, opening my eyes to look into hers.

She was looking back at me and she gave me a little smile.

"I know."

Of course it pretty much had to be Josette who moved out since my dad owned the house, but I wasn't going to let her go unless we found something decent. We started looking the very next day, perusing notice boards at the student union and several sites online.

"I'm actually hoping for another male flatmate," Josette mentioned as I peered over her shoulder at an ad. "I'm pretty pleased with how things worked out with my first one."

"Um-hmm," I said dryly, and I rested my chin on the top of her head.

I didn't like anything we looked at, and by the third day Josette forbid me to go with her anymore.

"You're too picky," she explained after I'd nixed yet another apartment.

"Nothing's been good enough yet," I argued.

"I'll find something I like and then you can give it your final approval," she suggested.

I frowned at the idea but grudgingly went along with it.

She found something the very next day and I went to look at it with her on Friday. It was nicer than my place but I still didn't think it was good enough for her. I grumbled about a floorboard that squeaked, insisting that there was probably dry rot in the floor joists.

She shook her head and rolled her eyes.

I continued checking things out while she went into the kitchen to sign a rental agreement with Patricia, her new landlord and roommate . . . er, flatmate. Both of them came running when I pushed the test button on the fire alarm.

"Marco!" Josette scolded, hitting me lightly on the arm.

"Do you have carbon monoxide detectors?" I asked Patricia, ignoring Josette, who rolled her eyes at me again.

"Just one," Patricia said, pointing. "It's by the back door."

"Marco," Josette complained, after Patricia headed back into the kitchen. "*You* don't even have a carbon monoxide detector!"

"I've been planning on getting one."

She raised an eyebrow at me and put a hand on her hip.

I looked at her for a moment.

"I'm sorry," I finally said quietly. "I just really don't want you to move out."

"I know," she whispered, stepping closer to me.

"And I want to make sure you're going to be all right," I went on softly. "I want to take care of you."

"You've been taking care of me since the day we met," she smiled, and she wrapped her arms around me and held me tight.

The next day, even though it was chilly, Josette and I went to the beach and had another picnic. After we had finished eating, I produced a small package and held it out toward her.

"Happy one-week anniversary," I said.

"One-week anniversary?"

I nodded.

"Does this mean you're going to give me something every Saturday?" she laughed, taking the package from me.

"Yes."

She smiled.

"Oh!" she said after she opened it. "This is the same perfume I wore last week!"

"I know," I said. "I called Brenda and asked her what kind it was. You were sitting right there next to her at the desk and didn't even know it."

She smiled again.

"You didn't know," I said worriedly, "did you?"

"No," she said, shaking her head and laughing.

She took the bottle out of the box it was in and spritzed some on one wrist and then rubbed her wrists together.

"I love the way this smells," she said, holding a wrist up to her nose. She extended it to me. "Do you like it?"

"It reminds me of our first date," I said. "So yes."

"Our *second* date," she corrected me, squirting some perfume on her neck.

"The first one didn't count."

"But you like it?"

"That smell will always remind me of the first time I kissed you," I said, "so, yes. I love it."

She smiled again.

"Here, let me smell," I said, leaning forward and putting my hands around her waist. I pulled her toward me and burrowed my face into her neck.

She squealed as I kissed her, but then I pulled away quickly, sputtering and wiping my mouth on my sleeve.

"Yuck!" I said. "That tastes awful!"

"Well you're not supposed to *taste* it!" she chided.

I continued sputtering and wiping while Josette laughed. When the taste was finally gone I looked at her. She was smiling and her eyes were still laughing.

"I like it when you laugh," I said seriously, reaching up and touching her cheek.

She looked at me appreciatively and I ran my hand along her lip.

She smiled.

"And I like it when you smile," I went on.

"You make me happy," she answered simply.

"Good," I replied, bringing her lips toward mine. "You make me happy, too."

I helped Josette move out the next day after church. It didn't take very long to transfer all of her worldly possessions, and after she had arranged what few items she owned the way she wanted in her new room, we said goodbye to Patricia and quickly headed back (to what was now just my place) for dinner.

After we cooked linguini and toasted garlic bread, Josette and I took our usual places on the couch, eating in front of the television and watching *Chances Are*, like we always had. Josette was so quiet for most of the show, however, that by the time the final bonus round rolled around, there was no way she was going to be able to beat me.

"What is the incongruous name of this poisonous woody vine, a member of the nightshade family?" Wally Fletcher asked. Photos of a plant I'd never seen before flashed up on the screen. It had reddish oval berries and purple flowers, and I had absolutely no idea what it was.

"Bittersweet," Josette said softly.

"Bittersweet," one of the contestants answered.

"Congratulations," Wally announced. "That is correct."

Josette turned to face me.

"That's how I feel," she said quietly. "Bittersweet."

I wrapped my arms around her and pulled her close.

"I know that the only reason we're having to do this is because things are going so great between us," she went on, looking up at me, "but I'm going to miss you so much."

"You're going to see me every single day," I reminded her, giving her a squeeze.

"It's not going to be the same . . ."

"The only difference is that we're not going to be sleeping under the same roof anymore," I pointed out.

"But I *like* sleeping under the same roof with you!" she cried, pulling back to look at me unhappily. "And that's *not* the only difference. I'm not going to see you in the morning when I get up or when I get home from school, and I'm not going to be able to say goodnight to you after I've finished brushing my teeth . . ."

We studied each other for a moment until I asked her quietly, "Do you want to stay?"

I absolutely would have let her if she'd said, "Yes."

"No," she said, shaking her head. "I mean I *do*, but I can't. I need to go."

"It's going to be okay."

"I'm going to miss you so much," she told me one more time.

"Things are only going to get better," I promised.

That week the two of us settled into a new routine. In the mornings, I would pick her up and take her to breakfast before dropping her off in time for her first class. A few hours later we would meet back up for lunch, buying something from the cafeteria or eating leftovers from dinner the night before. Once we were both ready to leave campus, I would pick her up again and we'd head to my place, where we would spend the rest of the evening together: cooking, eating, and watching TV . . . among other things.

The following Saturday we spent the entire day at St. Kilda. It was chilly again but by far the nicest day I had ever spent there. I loved walking around with the prettiest girl in all of Australia, holding hands with her and kissing her whenever I wanted.

That evening we returned to my house. Josette immediately sat down on the couch and picked up the remote to search for the latest episode of our show that had recorded while we'd been out. As she got it started, I stepped into my bedroom to retrieve a tightly wrapped package and presented it to her when I returned to the living room.

"Happy two-week anniversary," I said.

"I can't believe you're going to give me something every Saturday," she said, pausing Wally in mid-sentence with the remote.

"I can stop if you want."

"No, no," she replied, taking it from me. "I wasn't complaining."

She opened it and held up what was inside.

"It's an umbrella," she stated.

"And to think I was beginning to doubt your intellect."

"You were beginning to doubt my intellect?"

"No."

The umbrella was covered with words and she immediately started to open it to see what it said.

"It's bad luck to open an umbrella inside!" I cried, reaching my hand out to stop her.

"I don't believe in luck," she replied.

I didn't either. I smiled at her as she popped it open and started reading the passage that began in the center of the umbrella, spiraling around and around until it reached the very edge.

For, though shy, he did not seem reserved; it had rather the appearance of feelings glad to burst their usual restraints; and having talked of poetry, the richness of the present age, and gone through a brief comparison of opinion as to the first-rate poets, trying to ascertain whether Marmion or The Lady of the Lake were to be preferred, and how ranked the Giaour and The Bride of Abydos; and moreover, how the Giaour was to be pronounced, he showed himself so intimately acquainted with all the tenderest songs of the one poet, and all the impassioned descriptions of hopeless agony of the other; he repeated, with such tremulous feeling, the various lines which imaged a broken heart, or a mind destroyed by wretchedness, and looked so entirely as if he meant to be understood, that she ventured to hope he did not always read only poetry, and to say, that she thought it was the misfortune of poetry to be seldom safely enjoyed by those who enjoyed it completely; and that the strong feelings which alone could estimate it truly were the very feelings which ought to taste it but sparingly.

"Jane Austen wrote it," I said proudly. "That's her longest sentence ever. A hundred and ninety-three words."

She looked at me with her mouth slightly open.

"It's from *Persuasion*," I added. "Your favorite."

"I . . . I know," she said. "But . . . did you *write* this?"

I nodded.

"But it's so perfect!" she exclaimed. "How did you space it out like that so that it came out exactly right and everything?"

"Simple math," I said, shrugging. "I calculated the surface area and divided by how many characters there were – almost eleven hundred including all of her stupid semicolons – and then I just divided and that gave me almost nine square centimeters for each letter."

She laughed. "How many umbrellas did you go through trying to make this?"

"Including this one? Four."

"You are *so* sweet," she said, leaning forward and kissing me on the lips. "I love it."

"Speaking of anniversary presents," I said, sniffing, "I noticed earlier that you're wearing your perfume again. Does that mean that you don't want me kissing your neck?"

"It's not on my neck," she answered mischievously.

"Where'd you put it?"

"Nowhere you're going to be kissing," she said. "At least not tonight."

"Is that a challenge?"

She giggled and shook her head.

"Sounds like a challenge to me," I argued, and I moved toward her.

"No!" she shrieked as I dove to attack.

Josette squealed with laughter. The umbrella clattered to the floor.

She may have moved out, but the fact remained that Josette and I still had the entire house to ourselves anytime we wanted, and there really wasn't anything to stop the two of us from doing whatever we wanted. Both of us knew that it was only a matter of time before we were going to need to establish some self-imposed boundaries, or pretty soon we were going to get ourselves into trouble. In the meantime, though, I didn't worry about it. I just enjoyed kissing her.

~ ~ ~

JOSETTE AND I were planning to eat lunch together on Monday as we usually did, but she texted me about an hour before we were supposed to meet and told me that she was running late. She said she would stop by the lab and get me as soon as she could, and I told her to hurry up because I was hungry.

Everyone else in my research group went on to lunch, so by the time Josette snuck up behind me and covered my eyes with her hands, I was the only one left in the room.

"Guess who?" she asked.

"I don't know," I answered, "but my girlfriend's supposed to be here any minute so you'd better get out of here before she catches you."

"Aww, I'm not afraid of her," Josette said, leaning down and kissing my neck.

"I am," I replied, and she laughed, wheeling my chair around so that I was facing her. I put my hands on her hips and pulled her toward me, kissing her lips.

It was a rather fast kiss because it was so late and because I was so hungry. I'm not saying that it wasn't a nice kiss, I'm just saying that it wasn't magical and that it didn't give me butterflies in my stomach.

We were comfortable with each other now, and it was just a regular kiss.

If I'd known what was about to happen, I would have made more out of it.

~ ~ ~

AT LUNCH WE started arguing about whether we should take a vegetable tray or brownies to the covered dish lunch at church on Wednesday evening.

"We can take most of them with us," I said, rooting hard for the brownie idea, "but save a few out for ourselves."

"Yeah, right," she scoffed. "I know what 'a few' means coming from your mouth. We're going to wind up taking about *five* to the dinner."

"We can make two batches."

"Or we can just do vegetables," she said again.

"Why don't we do brownies *and* vegetables?" I suggested.

"Because we don't need to be eating a bunch of brownies!"

"We won't," I insisted. "We'll take most of them to church."

"Um-hmm," she said skeptically.

"All this talk about brownies is making me think some dessert is in order," I said, looking past her shoulder to the wall where the menus were posted.

She didn't answer me and I vaguely noticed that she was looking over my shoulder as well, to the door that led out of the cafeteria.

"You want a milkshake?" I asked. "Or do you want some of mine?"

She didn't answer.

I waited for her to make some comment about how unfair it was that I could drink ten milkshakes a day and never gain a pound but all she had to do was take one spoonful of mine and she wouldn't be able to fit into her jeans the next day.

She still didn't answer me, however, her eyes staying focused on something just past my shoulder.

"Josie?" I asked. "Do you want one or not?"

I watched as her mouth slowly dropped open and her eyes widened in silent shock.

"What's wrong?" I asked, but before I could turn around to see what Josette was staring at, someone spoke from behind me.

"Hace tiempo que no te veo, Marco."

Long time, no see, Marco.

Bizzy.

I felt my own eyes widen and I turned around.

"Bizzy?"

She was holding her cane in one hand and had her other hand on the arm of Jason, an undergraduate who worked in the lab two doors down from mine. She smiled that beautiful smile of hers.

"I told you I thought he was here," Jason said to her.

"Thank you," she said. She took her hand off his arm.

"No problem," he said, giving me and Josette a little wave before he turned and left.

I stood up and turned my back on Josette to face Bizzy.

"Bizzy," I said. "What are you *doing* here?"

"I wanted to surprise you," she said, still smiling.

"Well . . . congratulations."

She continued to smile and obviously expected a hug or something so I gave her one. After we pulled away from one another, she turned her face toward Josette. I don't have a clue how Bizzy knew she was there.

"I'm Bizzy," she said, extending her hand. Josette stood up.

"I'm Josette." They shook hands.

"Oh," Bizzy said. "Marco's roommate. It's so nice to meet you."

"It's nice to meet you, too," Josette said, reaching for her purse. "Well, I'd better get going."

I wanted to tell her not to go, but I just stood there, speechless, barely able to believe what was happening.

"Please don't go on my account," Bizzy said, losing her smile for the first time.

"No, no," Josette said. "I need to get going. Have a nice visit."

"Thank you," Bizzy said, her face following the sound of Josette's footsteps as she headed quickly toward the door.

"I hope she didn't leave just because of me," Bizzy said, turning toward me again.

"What are you doing here, Bizzy?" I asked, finally finding my voice.

She was quiet for a moment before she answered me softly.

"I thought about what you said," she eventually said. "And I was wrong. We love each other and we should be together. I shouldn't have put you off."

My voice left me again.

"But I won't put you off anymore," she said, standing before me expectantly.

It took a minute before I wasn't speechless anymore, before I could say, "We need to go somewhere where we can talk."

It was then that the first look of doubt crossed her face.

"Am I too late?" she asked softly.

I looked at her for another moment and pressed my lips together.

"I'm sorry," I said, reaching out to take her hand.

She closed her eyes and pressed her own lips together, shaking her head slightly and then turning her face from me.

After a moment she took a deep breath, opened her eyes, and turned toward me again.

"Let's sit down," I suggested. The middle of the cafeteria wasn't necessarily the best place to have this conversation, but I could tell that Bizzy wasn't exactly going to fall apart or anything.

We sat and I told her I was really sorry again and gave her hand a reassuring squeeze.

"It's okay," she finally said, squeezing my hand in return.

"I . . . I don't know what to say," I told her.

"You don't have to say anything," she said. "It's my own fault."

"No—" I started to argue, but she cut me off.

"Grace told me I was an idiot," she said.

"Grace?"

146

Bizzy nodded. "When she got back from her honeymoon, I told her that you'd proposed to me, and she said I was being stupid. She said I was never going to find anybody who was as good of a person as you are and that I was making a huge mistake if I let you get away."

"*Grace* said that?"

She nodded.

I shook my head in disbelief.

"Why is it too late?" she wanted to know.

I was quiet.

"Is there someone else?" Bizzy asked.

This time I answered. "Yes."

"Is it Josette?" Bizzy asked, nodding in the direction Josette had headed off.

I hesitated for a moment but then, very quietly, answered, "Yes."

She pursed her lips one more time and shook her head again.

"Nothing was going on before," I said hastily.

"How long have you been seeing her?"

"Two weeks."

She thought about that for a moment.

"And you're already serious about her?"

"Yes."

"How serious?"

"I love her."

How odd it was that I was sitting here telling Bizzy that I loved Josette when I hadn't even told *Josette* that I loved Josette.

Suddenly I couldn't wait to find her and let her know.

"That seems awfully fast," Bizzy observed.

"Nothing was going on," I promised again. Then I added, "But I have known her for almost a year. We already knew each other pretty well."

Bizzy sighed in resignation.

"I'm really sorry," I repeated earnestly.

"It's okay," she assured me. "I'll be okay."

"I know you will be," I smiled. "I've never worried about that."

She gave me a small, appreciative smile of her own.

"Are you hungry?" I asked.

"No," she answered, shaking her head.

"What's your schedule?"

"I wasn't sure how long I'd be here, so I got an open-ended ticket," she explained. "I guess I'll probably go back tomorrow."

"No," I argued. "You can't come all the way to Australia and only stay for *one* day. You need to hang around."

"I don't—" she began, shaking her head.

"I know a place we can go where you can stick your hand inside of a kangaroo's pouch," I interrupted.

"Stick your hand inside a kangaroo's pouch?" she repeated slowly.

"Uh-huh."

"Isn't that kind of weird?"

"Possibly," I grinned.

She smiled back.

"You don't think your new girlfriend's going to have a problem with you spending a bunch of time with your *old* girlfriend?"

"Nah," I said, feeling myself smile again. "That's one thing about Josie. She doesn't sweat the small stuff."

A few hours later I dropped Bizzy off at her hotel with the promise that I'd be back in time to pick her up for dinner.

She wanted to clean up and rest up.

I wanted to see Josette.

On the drive over to her apartment, I thought how strange it was that Josette and I hadn't said "I love you" to each other, but I knew that she loved me just as much as I loved her. I felt more loved by Josette – even though she had never said it once – than I had ever felt loved by Bizzy – even though Bizzy used to say it all the time.

Like I said before . . . everything is upside down in Australia.

148

AS I PARKED in front of Josette's new apartment, I found myself wishing that I'd stopped and gotten flowers or redeemed my credit at the jewelry store or something. I couldn't wait any longer to see Josette though, and I jumped out of my car and took the steps to her apartment two at a time.

When I arrived at her door, I knocked and stood in the hallway outside, rocking anxiously back and forth on my heels. After what seemed like a very long moment, Josette finally opened the door.

She looked horrible.

There was no "Hello." No hug. No trace of a smile.

Just sadness.

I looked at her in surprise. Was she honestly worried that I might choose Bizzy over her? Did she not have a clue how I felt about her?

"I love you," I said. "I love you more than anything on this earth. I don't know why I haven't told you that already and I'm sorry, but I love you and you're the only person I ever want to be with."

I was expecting my hug or a smile or something at this point, but she didn't move.

"I didn't know she was coming," I said quickly. "I told her right away that I loved you and that she was too late."

"You shouldn't have done that, Marco," Josette said quietly, and she dropped her eyes to the floor.

"Of course I should have," I said. "Didn't you hear what I just said? I love you . . . not Bizzy. *You.*"

She was silent for another moment and then she lifted her head and looked me in the eyes.

"Stuart called," she said.

"What?"

"I said, 'Stuart called'."

I looked at her, uncomprehending. It took a very long moment for it all to register, but when it did, I slowly started shaking my head.

"No," I said, shaking harder.

"About two hours ago," she replied, nodding in return. "He wants to try to work things out."

"You're getting a divorce," I protested.

"Two more weeks and it would have been finalized," she agreed. "But he wants to get back together."

"No," I said again, shaking my head more.

She looked at me unhappily and didn't say anything.

"You can't go back to him," I said desperately.

"I *have* to," she answered. "He's my *husband*."

"Is that what you want?" I asked, incredulous.

"This isn't about what I want," she said forcefully. "He's my husband."

I stared at her, hoping that this was all just some big lie she'd concocted to get even with me because Bizzy had shown up or something.

But it wasn't.

"What about that girl he was living with?" I asked.

"I guess they broke up."

"You *guess*?"

"They . . . they did. They broke up."

"Why?"

"I don't know," she said, now sounding flustered. "They just broke up."

"And so he suddenly wants to get back together with you and you're just fine with everything?"

"It doesn't matter if I'm fine with it or not," she answered impatiently. "This is what God wants me to do and it's what I'm going to do."

"How do you know it's what God wants you to do?" I asked.

"Because," she cried, waving her hand in the air, her voice rising. "It says in the Bible that if a woman has an unbelieving husband and he's willing to live with her, then she's not supposed to divorce him."

150

I wanted to shake my head at her again, but I couldn't.

"And besides," she added quietly, "that's why He brought Bizzy to you today."

"No."

"Yes, Marco," Josette insisted. "It's not a coincidence that she showed up *today* of all days. God knows that Bizzy's who you're supposed to be with and Stuart's who I'm supposed to be with and He's working everything out for both of us."

"No," I said again.

"Look," she said softly. "I know this might not be what you want right now, but one day you're going to look back on this and see that God was in control and that He knew what was best for you all along."

"*You're* what's best for me."

She looked at me miserably for another moment but then took a step backward into her apartment.

"You need to go, Marco. Go find Bizzy and make things right with her." And then Josette stepped all the way back into her new apartment and closed the door in my face.

~ ~ ~

REMEMBER HOW PLEASED I was with myself when Bizzy broke up with me and I discovered that my faith was so strong?

What a crock.

~ ~ ~

I WAS AN adulterer.

Jesus said that if you lust after a woman, you've already committed adultery with her in your heart.

I thought about Josette all the time.

I missed her touch and her scent and her laugh and her smile and her company and her warmth and her kisses and her hugs and her voice and everything about her. I missed her with an ache that wouldn't go away.

Every night I stole into Josette's old room and curled up on the futon, closing my eyes in the darkness and trying to pretend that she wasn't gone. I went to the department store and bought a bottle of the same perfume I'd given her on our one-week anniversary, and I set it on my nightstand or the kitchen windowsill or the bathroom counter – wherever I was going to be – and I opened it to inhale memories of her and to make myself miss her even more.

I thought about Stuart constantly too, and I hated him. I hated him for every heartache he had ever caused her and I hated him for taking her away from me and I hated him for being her husband and for sleeping next to her and for making love to her every night.

Anyone who hates his brother is a murderer . . .

So I was that too.

I came home one evening and found that Josette had been there during the day while I was gone. She'd left four items on the little table in the kitchen: her copy of the key to my house, the umbrella, the perfume, and the copy of *Persuasion* that I'd given her for Christmas.

That night I curled up on the futon and began reading. Jane Austen wasn't any easier to understand now than she'd been when I was in high school, but I forced myself to plow forward every night until I finished the book that Josette loved so much. It was the story of Anne and Wentworth – two people who loved each other desperately but spent years apart before they were finally able to be together. When I was finally finished, I fantasized that Josette had left it on the table for me as a message: *We're apart right now, but one day we'll find our way back to each other . . .*

I'd been to the main library only one time since Josette had left, going there to talk to Brenda (and finding out that all she knew was that Josette had quit her work-study job and moved back in with her husband). But after I read *Persuasion*, I went back again and again, perusing the shelves and desperately searching for other novels that Josette had told me about. I racked my brain, trying to recall titles of the different ones she had mentioned to me and reading each one after I found it.

I read books by George Eliot, Compton Mackenzie, Tom Wolfe, C.S. Lewis, and Harper Lee. I imagined what Josette's thoughts had been as she'd read the very same words I was reading, and I searched for the escape that Josette's mother had once told her about.

But I never found it.

That didn't stop me from trying though. I went back to the library week after week, and I devoured book after book.

I may have been an adulterer and a murderer . . .
But at least I was well-read.

~ ~ ~

I WAS LOSING my dad, too.

For my entire life, Dad had been fixing things for me whenever something went wrong.

Right after Josette had closed the door in my face, I'd called him, knowing that he would somehow be able to make everything better again. But the man who answered his phone was a complete stranger to me, and apparently I was a stranger to him, too.

"He's getting a bit worse," Mom had admitted quietly after she'd taken the phone from Dad.

She promised to have him call me when he was more himself (it comes and goes, she'd said), but I knew that my days of turning to him for help were over.

I went home for Christmas and was glad to find that Dad was indeed still having good moments, but I didn't dare burden him or Mom with my troubles. Instead, I mentioned to Mom that maybe I should think about moving in with them after I finished my degree the following summer. It was obvious that she was going to be needing help soon, and – even though the company our program partnered with had already offered to turn my internship into a full-time position – I really couldn't see myself staying in Australia. Mom said that we could think about it and that she would pray about it. She told me that I should pray about it too . . . that I should see what God wanted me to do.

I didn't have the heart to tell her that I couldn't even begin to pray. Did God really want to hear me begging Him to send a married woman back into my arms?

I didn't think so.

I kept quiet.

~ ~ ~

I WAS DEPRESSED.

After I got back to Australia I went to a doctor and *told* him I was depressed. He wanted to know if I was suicidal.

Well, duh.

Why did he think I was there if it wasn't because I was scared about the way things were headed? He sent me on my way with a prescription for a medication that didn't help and an appointment with a counselor that didn't help either.

That was when I realized that even the science I loved so much couldn't save me . . .

And I grew even more scared.

~ ~ ~

EVEN THOUGH MY faith was shot, I was smart enough to know that I had no hope if I didn't do something to fix my relationship with God.

I had no idea how to do that though . . . no idea how to reach Him. I tried to pray, but I just couldn't.

I did manage, however, to send a text to my sister Lily. *Will you please pray for me?*
She texted me back immediately: *Do you want to talk?*
No.
Okay, she answered. *I'm praying.*

Of all my siblings, Lily was the one who was the most like me. I wasn't closest to her by any means, but I had the most in common with her. Dorito and Lily and I were all Latino and had been raised by white parents, but only Lily and I had been abandoned at birth because there was something wrong with us. We were also the only two who didn't know our birth moms. More than that, though, was the fact that Lily was so much like me personality-wise. We were both quiet and reserved. Introverted and serious.

And I knew that I could trust Lily.

I knew that I could send her a text asking for prayer and that she wouldn't freak out. I knew that she wasn't going to get on the phone and babble to everyone in the family that something was going on. I knew that she wasn't going to pepper me with questions, bugging me to let her know what was wrong. Of course she might ask me if I wanted to talk, but I knew that she would butt out when I told her that I didn't.

Apparently I knew nothing.

Lily called two days after my text and told me she was coming to visit.

"No."

"Marco," she insisted, "Mom said you're thinking about moving home this summer? This is my last chance to come to Australia and have a free place to stay."

(Another thing we had in common was that she was just about as bad of a liar as I was.)

"No, Lily," I said firmly. "I do *not* want you over here hounding me with questions and trying to get me to talk. I thought you were the *one* person in my life I could ask to pray for me without worrying that you were going to start prying."

"Who's prying?" she asked innocently. "I want to see a koala bear."

"No."

"Marco," she said gently. "I won't pry. I want to come see you, but we don't have to talk. I promise."

"No," I said again, my resolve much weaker this time. "I don't want you to come."

"Well, I'm coming anyway," she said adamantly. "I already bought my ticket and it's nonrefundable. I fly into Tullamarine Saturday morning at ten-thirteen. If you're not there to pick me up I guess I'll just have to get a taxi and find a hotel and show myself around."

I didn't say anything.

"Gate eleven," she said quietly.

I still didn't answer her.

"Goodbye, Marco."

I did not *want* to talk to Lily about what was going on. I didn't want to talk to anybody about what was going on (which, incidentally, was why counseling hadn't gone too great), but as soon as I saw Lily on Saturday morning, I knew that I was going to do nothing *but* talk . . . and as soon as I hugged her, I started crying.

"It's okay," Lily whispered in my ear, hugging me back.

"No, it's not," I answered, wiping my eyes before taking her hand and leading her away to baggage claim.

I started talking on the ride back to my house, and I kept it up for the next three days. I talked at the wildlife sanctuary and at St. Kilda Beach and at Fitzroy Gardens. I talked at restaurants. I talked in the living room and in the kitchen and on the front porch, and some nights I knocked on Josette's old door and sat down on the edge of the futon where Lily was now sleeping and I talked some more.

I talked and I talked and I talked, and sometimes I cried.

And Lily listened.

One day Lily and I were both crying because we were talking about Dad. Lily mentioned that – during the times when he was still himself – he had been busy planning his funeral.

"What do you mean?" I asked.

"You know," she explained, "like he's been working with me and Meredith on this photo montage he wants and making sure we know what song he wants played and stuff like that."

"What song does he want?"

"'Revelation Song'," she answered.

"Why?"

"I don't know," she shrugged. Then she lowered her voice to imitate Dad and shook a finger at me sternly. "But it needs to be the one by Phillips, Craig and Dean."

I looked at her questioningly.

"It's very important that we get the Phillips, Craig and Dean version," she said with a tearful smile. "Don't let me forget, okay? It's very important that I *don't* forget."

"I gather he's mentioned it a few times?"

"A few dozen," she nodded, and we both smiled through our tears.

That night I lay in bed, wondering why Dad wanted "Revelation Song" played at his funeral. I knew he liked it – I remembered him turning up the radio whenever it came on and singing along at the top of his lungs, not worrying for one second about how his voice sounded or how much he might be embarrassing us kids. But he had done that with a lot of songs, so that didn't really explain why it was the one he wanted played at his funeral.

I tried to remember the words to "Revelation Song," but I couldn't. I looked them up online and after I'd read them, I puzzled over his choice even more. I pulled out my Bible and turned to the book of Revelation, flipping pages until my eyes found the verse that was used as the opening line in the song: *Worthy is the Lamb, who was slain.*

I continued scanning and found the passage that was used in the chorus: *Holy, holy, holy is the Lord God Almighty, who was, and is, and is to come . . .*

Reading on, I found verses about rainbows and lightning and thunder, and before long I realized that most of the words in the song had come directly from the book of Revelation (which I guess kind of made sense since it was called "Revelation Song").

But that still didn't explain why Dad wanted it played at his funeral.

For someone my age, I had actually been to a lot of funerals. My sister Meredith had lost a friend in a car accident. My grandmothers had both died and so had my brother-in-law's mother. A teacher from my school had passed away from a heart attack. A classmate of mine and Grace's had died from cancer.

I thought now about some of the songs I remembered from those funerals and from things I'd seen on TV or whatever.

Go Rest High on that Mountain . . . I Can Only Imagine . . . I'll Fly Away . . . Amazing Grace . . . Beulah Land . . . I Will Rise . . .

Those were common funeral songs. They were about leaving the sorrows of this life behind and going to a wonderful new life. They were songs about meeting Jesus.

But "Revelation Song"?

I got up and knocked on Lily's door. When she didn't answer, I knew that she was already in bed and had taken her cochlear implants off. I cracked the door and when I still didn't hear anything from her, I reached my hand into the room and flashed the light on and off.

She sat up.

"Sorry," I mouthed.

"Hey, *Muñeco*," she said softly, reaching for one of the receivers that was charging on the nightstand. She secured it in place while I sat down on the edge of the futon. Once she could hear me, she asked, "What's up?"

"I think I figured out why Dad wants 'Revelation Song' played at his funeral."

"Why?"

"All the songs you usually hear at funerals are about people going to heaven, right?"

"Yeah . . . so?"

"But 'Revelation Song' is about Jesus. It's all about worshiping Him and how He's holy and worthy and everything . . ."

"Okay . . ."

She looked at me blankly.

"Dad doesn't want the focus to be on him," I explained. "He wants the focus to be on Jesus."

She thought about that for a moment and then nodded.

"Yeah," she agreed. "I can see that."

I scooted across the futon until my back was against the wall and I sighed. Lily waited.

"I thought I was like that," I finally said quietly. "I thought I was right where I needed to be, you know?"

Lily gave me a little nod and put her hand on my knee.

"I mean, I went to church every Sunday and I was reading my Bible every day and I listened to only Christian music and . . ."

My voice trailed off.

"I thought my faith was strong," I said.

Lily continued to listen.

162

I shrugged. "When Bizzy broke up with me, I did fine. I mean, I just figured that God had someone else in mind for me, you know?"

I glanced at her and she nodded.

"I thought the reason I handled everything so well was because of my *faith*," I said, "but it was really just because – deep down – I knew that Bizzy wasn't the right one for me."

I looked away and shook my head.

"I mean, for our entire relationship I was always worried that I wasn't good enough for Bizzy," I continued, "or I was nervous that she was going to break up with me, or I was scared that she didn't feel the same way about me that I felt about her . . ."

I glanced at Lily again.

"It didn't have anything to do with my faith," I said miserably. "My faith was a sham."

"No," Lily said, shaking her head. "It wasn't a sham."

"Then where is it now?" I challenged. "I don't have faith that things are going to get better now."

I shook my own head and turned away from her, trying to blink back the tears that were coming once more.

I was *so* far away from God . . .

I started to cry.

I was far away from God and I had no idea how to get back to Him. He was as out of reach for me as Josette was.

Lily scooted so that she was next to me and she wrapped her arms around me.

She prayed for me.

And she held me while I cried.

~ ~ ~

UP UNTIL THAT point, Lily had mostly been listening. She hadn't given me a lot of advice or judged me or told me what I needed to do.

That changed the next day, however, the day before she was scheduled to leave.

"I want to talk to you," she said as soon as I walked into the living room that morning. She was sitting on the couch, waiting for me.

"Okay," I said slowly, stepping into the kitchen and heading for the coffeepot. She waited until I got my coffee and joined her on the couch.

"What do you want to talk about?" I asked, looking at her expectantly.

"I have something for you," she said, reaching beside her and picking up a book. She handed it to me.

"*John*," I said, reading the cover out loud. "*The Beloved Disciple*."

I looked at the author.

"Beth Moore?" I frowned.

"I know you think she just writes for women," Lily said quickly, holding a hand out as if to stop me from handing the book back, "but I think this is exactly what you need right now."

I looked at her doubtfully.

"She only calls her readers 'girlfriend', like, maybe one time," Lily promised, and I rolled my eyes.

"I think a huge part of your problem," she went on, undeterred, "is that all you're letting yourself think about is Josette."

I couldn't argue with that.

"She's *married*, Marco," Lily said gently. "It's not good for you to be thinking about her all the time."

"I can't help it."

164

"Yes, you can," she argued. "You know what Mom always says . . ."

You can't keep birds from flying over your head, but that doesn't mean you need to let them make nests in your hair.

I rolled my eyes again.

"I don't think Mom has any idea what it's like to be in love with someone that you shouldn't be in love with," I said dryly.

"Maybe not," Lily admitted, "but the fact of the matter is that *you're* in control of where your mind goes. I'm not saying that you're never going to think about Josette, but that doesn't mean you need to let your thoughts *dwell* on her. You need to stay focused on something else."

"Like this?" I asked sarcastically, holding up the book.

"It's really good," she insisted, "and I think it'll help you get your mind back where it needs to be."

Somehow I doubted that, but I gave her a polite little nod.

"Focus on *this*, Marco," she said, tapping the book. "YOU are in control of what you do and where your mind goes. Make yourself read it, every day. Okay?"

I nodded at her reluctantly.

"Promise?" she asked, and I nodded again.

~ ~ ~

NO BOOK WAS going to fix things for me . . . I was sure of that. But – because I had promised – I started reading about the beloved disciple the day after Lily flew home.

Some people have a mountaintop experience – a watershed moment in their lives where suddenly everything changes, God reveals who He is to them, and their relationship with Him is great from then on.

That's not at all how it happened with me.

I didn't read Lily's book and find myself miraculously transported to the top of a mountain, marveling at God's splendor and sovereignty.

I had to *climb* that mountain – step by step – and it took a very long time.

But it was while reading that book that I finally found the escape Josette's mother had talked about. And it was while reading that book that I finally started thinking about something besides Josette.

My first step.

Lily checked up on me regularly. Naturally she was pleased to find out that I was reading (and actually enjoying) the book she'd given me, yet she was horrified to find out that it was the *only* thing I'd been reading.

It probably comes as no surprise that I hadn't read my Bible since the day I lost Josette, but in reality I had started slipping away from that habit even *before* she'd left . . . during the short time we'd dated. Several mornings I had awakened and grabbed my computer instead of my Bible, using my normal reading time instead to go online to look for umbrellas or perfume or apartments with carbon monoxide detectors. Other mornings, I had opened my Bible – intending to read – but my mind had almost immediately drifted off to thoughts about Josette and the last time I had kissed her or the next time I was going to.

That was when my focus had first started getting off track.

"You have *got* to start reading the Bible again," Lily scolded me now. And she pestered and hounded me until I promised her that I'd read that every day, too.

A second step.

Lily also chided me about going back to church. She reminded me that I was in control of what went into my mind, and she convinced me that going back to church was another opportunity to focus on God.

And so I went back.

The Sunday School class greeted me enthusiastically with huge smiles and hugs when I walked through the door. Naturally they asked me about Josette, but if they suspected that the two of us had ever become anything more than friends, they didn't let on when I told them where she was.

They didn't pry.

They just nodded understandingly and promised me that they were praying, and then they swept me right up in their lesson.

A third step.

I wasn't anywhere close to where I needed to be . . . I wasn't even close to where I'd once been . . .

But by the time nine months had gone by since I'd last seen Josette, at least I was headed in the right direction.

~ ~ ~

MY CAR NEEDED new tires.

I was going to sell it before I moved back to the States and I knew that it would go a lot quicker with better tires, so I dropped it off at a tire place on a drizzly Tuesday morning and hopped a bus to the university. That afternoon I took another bus back to pick it up, paid my bill and headed home, remembering that I needed to stop somewhere for shampoo and cereal.

I normally shopped at the grocery store near campus that I passed every day on my way home, but it wasn't on my way today. I hated shopping at other stores because it was always so hard to find anything, but when I saw a supermarket ahead and the light changed in my favor, I decided to pull in. I only needed two things . . . how long could it possibly take?

I parked and walked in, immediately spotting the produce section and grabbing a cart, deciding that I might as well pick up some bananas while I was there, too.

After I selected three that looked promising, I passed by the store's display of muntries. I let myself remember – for just a moment – the day Josette had led me into the backyard to show me all the little berries that covered my muntrie bush, but then I made myself move on.

All of a sudden, though, there she was . . .

And I couldn't move on.

She was right in front of me, and even though she had her back to me, I recognized her instantly. Her dark hair was piled on top of her head and she had one hand on her hip. She was weighing something and I knew without even seeing her face that she was biting her lip in concentration as she studied the numbers on the scale. The sight of her took my breath away, but somehow I actually managed to pray.

168

I asked God what He wanted me to do, fully expecting to hear Him say, *Run!*

But I didn't hear anything.

Nothing at all.

I stood and I watched.

And I kept praying.

But still, I heard nothing.

After what seemed like a very long while, I decided that I had given God plenty of time.

I walked up behind her.

"Josie."

She startled and turned to face me.

"Marco," she said in a whisper.

"Hi, Josie."

"Hi," she said, still whispering.

"How're you doing?"

She cleared her throat and nodded.

"Good," she said, finding her voice and bobbing her head. "I'm good."

"Good."

"How are you?" she asked.

"Good."

We stared at each other for a moment.

"What are you doing here?" she asked.

"I had to get new tires on my car," I said, motioning in the direction from which I had just come.

"Oh."

There was another moment of silence.

"You grew your moustache back," she finally said.

"Yeah," I nodded, reaching up and rubbing it. "I figured since Dad paid all that money for it I probably better have one."

"How's he doing?" she asked gently.

"Umm, he's getting worse," I admitted. "I went home at Christmas . . . I could definitely see a change."

"I'm sorry."

I nodded at her again.

"How's Stuart?" I asked.

She dropped her eyes and shook her head.

"What's wrong?"

She hesitated for a long moment before facing me again.

"He went back to Rebecca four weeks ago," she told me.

"He left you *again*?" I asked in disbelief.

She gave a tiny nod.

"Why didn't you tell me?" I cried.

"You . . . I thought you were back with Bizzy . . ."

"Why in the *world* would I be back with Bizzy?"

She didn't answer.

"I was going to *leave* at the end of next month," I cried. "I would have gotten on that plane and never would have seen you again! Why didn't you *call* me?"

She looked at me quietly for another moment and then said, "We need to go somewhere where we can talk."

Two minutes later we were sitting in the front seat of my car, our shopping carts abandoned in the produce section.

"Talk," I said.

She looked down at her lap and didn't say anything for a long time.

I didn't say anything either. I just waited.

Finally she looked back up at me.

"I'm twelve weeks pregnant."

I can handle that.

She looked away.

"Does Stuart know?" I asked gently.

"Yes."

"He knew you were pregnant and he still left you?"

She took a deep breath and let it out slowly.

"Rebecca's pregnant too," Josette said.

I stared at her in disbelief and then closed my eyes, leaning my head back against the seat and sighing.

"I hate him," I muttered under my breath.

"No," Josette said, reaching out and touching my arm. "Don't say that."

I opened my eyes to look at her and – when I did – she quickly took her hand away.

170

"I do," I said. "I hate him and I hate the way he treats you."

"Things have been hard for him–" she began, but I cut her off.

"Why are you making excuses for him?" I cried.

"Because," she said quietly. "I know what he's been through."

I shook my head in disgust and stared out the window.

"Please don't be mad," she said in a quiet voice.

"I'm not mad, Josie," I said gently, turning back to her. "But I care about you and I'm worried about you." I reached my hand out and rested it on her cheek. "And I love you . . ."

"I'm still married," she said, and I took my hand off her cheek.

"I'm sorry."

She nodded and stared out the front windshield.

"If he decides to stay with Rebecca this time," she said softly, "we'll be divorced in eleven months. If he wants to try to work things out with me between now and then . . ."

She paused before going on.

"Then I have to do everything I can to make that happen," she finished.

"And then Rebecca's going to be left to raise a baby all alone instead of you?" I asked. "How's that going to be a good situation?"

"I didn't say any of this was good," she answered, turning back to me. "I'm saying that I'm still married and he's still my husband and I can't forget that this time."

I stared at her for a long moment.

"Where are you staying?" I finally asked.

"About three blocks from here . . . just off of Nicholson."

"Let's go back in there and get the rest of your groceries," I suggested, nodding toward the store, "and then I'll drive you home."

"No," she said, shaking her head. "I'm taking the bus."

"That's ridiculous," I argued. "I'm right here. Let me drive you home."

"No. I don't think that's a good idea."

"Why not?"

"Didn't you hear what I just said?" she asked. "I'm married. I'm married, I'm married, I'm *married*."

"Married people can't have friends?"

She looked at me miserably.

"Nothing will happen," I vowed, holding up one hand. "We'll just be friends."

"No, Marco," she said, shaking her head. "We can't do that."

"Yes we can," I insisted.

"No."

"Please, Josie," I begged. "I know you. I know you're going to need help getting through this."

She didn't answer.

"Please? *Please* let me be your friend."

She looked at me dubiously.

"Just friends," I promised quietly. "Nothing will happen."

She hesitated and glanced down at her lap.

"You need a friend," I whispered, "just a friend."

She finally looked back up at me. And she nodded.

~ ~ ~

AS SOON AS I got home I called Lily.

"Ohhh, this is *not* a good idea," she said as soon as I'd filled her in on everything.

"We're just going to be friends . . ."

"You can't just be friends with her."

"Yes I can."

"You're skating on *very* thin ice."

"I can handle it," I assured her. "All I've got to do is get through the next eleven months."

"And what if God wants them to get back together?"

"Why would He want that?"

She sighed into the phone.

"Marco–" she began.

"I know, I know."

"I mean it, Marco," Lily said. "I don't like this at all. You're putting yourself in a very dangerous situation."

"I won't let anything happen," I promised.

"It's not going to be as easy as you think," Lily warned. "You two already have a history together and now you've got pregnancy hormones to worry about on top of everything else."

"Pregnancy hormones?"

"Yeah."

"You mean, like, she's going to be emotional and stuff?"

"No," Lily said. "I mean like she's going to be . . ."

"What?"

There was a long pause.

"I can't say it."

"Huh?"

"I can't say that word to my brother."

"What word?"

"Are you absolutely clueless, Marco?" she cried.

173

"What are you talking about?"

"I'm talking about how if Josette had to *move out* last time because the two of you couldn't keep your hands off each other, it's going to be a million times worse now."

"It is?"

"Yes."

"Really?"

"Yes!"

"Because of pregnancy hormones?"

"Yes."

"Why would pregnancy hormones do that?" I asked.

"I don't know, Marco, they just do."

"Are you sure about this?"

"Yes!" she shouted. "I'm sure!"

"But, I mean, from a biological standpoint, why would–"

"I don't *know*, Marco," she said again, cutting me off, "but I'm not having this conversation with you anymore. All I'm telling you is that if you insist on trying to be friends with her, you need to be very, very careful."

"Okay."

"And don't touch her."

"What?"

"I said, 'Don't touch her'."

"I can't *touch* her?"

"No."

"O-kay," I said slowly.

"And be super careful."

"Okay," I said again. "I promise. I'll be super careful."

~ ~ ~

NATURALLY I DIDN'T listen to Lily. I was fairly confident that Josette and I could *touch* each other. What could possibly be wrong with an innocent hug hello or a quick hug goodbye?

It only took about a week for that to unravel.

One evening I stopped by the library (where Brenda had managed to give Josette back her work-study position) to see if she would let me drive her home. She not only accepted but also agreed to let me take her out to eat – just as friends, of course.

We had a nice dinner together, talking about work and other things of no consequence, and afterward I drove her to her apartment. Our conversation turned to her new flatmate, Fran. I had only met Fran once, but she seemed to dislike me immensely and I mentioned this to Josette.

"I wouldn't take it too personally," Josette said. "I think she pretty much hates everyone."

"Even you?"

"Yeah. I think she'd rather live alone, but she can't afford it."

"Is she mean to you?" I asked worriedly.

"Not really."

I looked at her with concern.

"She's just rude," Josette assured me. "Don't worry about it. I can handle it."

We pulled in to the parking lot of their complex and I noticed that the lights were off in the apartment.

"Doesn't look like she's here," I said. "That's good, right?"

"It's not bad," she admitted.

"What does she do that's rude?" I asked as we headed up the stairs.

"I don't know." Josette shrugged. "If I leave a bowl or something on the counter and she sees it she'll let out this great big sigh and then slam it all dramatically into the sink like I'm the bane of her existence. And heaven forbid if I should need to use the bathroom while she's sleeping. She comes out in the hall and is all like, 'What are you *doing*?' and I'm like, 'Just flushing the toilet, Fran. Calm down'."

"Do you really say that?"

"No," Josette said, as we trudged up the steps to her landing. "But I feel like it."

"What do you say?"

"I just tell her I'm sorry and I scuttle back to my room."

"Why don't we find you somewhere else to live?" I suggested.

"Because I have a year-long lease," she replied with a sigh. "Year-long."

I sighed too.

"I don't like it," I said, shaking my head.

"It's okay, Marco," she said as we arrived at her door. "She's the least of my worries."

This made me look at her even more worriedly and she tried to lighten the mood.

"It's not that big of a deal," she assured me, laying her hand on my arm. "I'm just saying that she's not exactly the best flatmate I've ever had in my life, that's all."

I'm sure she hadn't meant anything by it, but both of us stopped and looked at each other much longer than we should have.

"Well, I . . . I'd better get going," she said hastily, removing her hand and looking down into her purse to find her keys.

She pulled them out and turned to unlock the door. Once she had it open she faced me again and said, "Thank you for dinner. I really appreciate it."

"No problem," I said, and I reached to give her one of those quick and innocent hugs.

But it wasn't quick. And then it wasn't innocent.

176

We didn't pull away from each other like we were supposed to. We lingered. My arms stayed around her waist . . . hers rested on my shoulders. And we stood there like that, just holding each other. Josette pressed her body even closer to mine and my pulse somehow quickened. I hesitated for only a second before pulling her tighter, and when I did, I could feel the gentle swell of her belly against me and her warm breath against my neck.

I buried my face in her hair, my mouth near her ear . . .

I could have whispered a million things.

We stood there like that for way too long. I thought about asking God to give me the strength to stop, but I didn't want to.

Instead, I whispered, "I love you."

I barely said it. My voice was so soft that I wasn't certain I actually had until she whispered back, "We can't do this."

But even as she said it, I felt her grip on me tighten, and I moved closer.

"I know."

"I have to go," she said. She was still whispering. Her breath was still warm against my neck.

"I know," I said again, nodding. "Go."

She nodded back but didn't move.

"Go," I urged again, this time loosening my hold on her slightly. She moved away, barely a fraction of an inch.

"I'm sorry," she said and I shook my head as she stepped further away, her eyes cast down to the floor. She backed into her apartment and glanced up at me before she shut the door. "I'm sorry," she said again, and then she was gone.

~ ~ ~

I DID *NOT* want to lose Josette again . . . at that point, I would have done anything to keep her in my life.

But I didn't want to lose God again either.

It had taken me *so* long to get to where I was with Him. Granted I still had a long way to go, but the thought of starting over again scared me . . . almost as much as the thought of losing Josette.

A man brought his little boy to Jesus to be healed. He asked Jesus, "If you can do anything, take pity on us and help us."

Jesus answered, "'*If* you can'? Everything is possible for one who believes."

The man responded by saying, "I do believe, help me overcome my unbelief!"

That was me.

I believed that God works all things to the good of those who love Him, but I didn't believe that He would work this out good for me.

I know I'm supposed to pray for Your will, but I'm scared of Your will. I want to want what You want, but not really. Not unless it's the same thing that I want . . .

Babbling honesty.

But once I finally told Him how I was really feeling, God showed me what He really wanted.

And after that, I wasn't so scared anymore.

Another step.

178

~ ~ ~

I WAS WAITING on Josette's landing the next day when she arrived home. She stopped climbing the stairs as soon as she saw me.

"I just want to talk to you for a second," I said, holding up my hands as if in surrender so that she wouldn't turn around and head the other way.

"We can't do this, Marco," she said, shaking her head.

"I just want to *talk* to you," I repeated.

She looked at me doubtfully but finished climbing the steps.

"Let's sit down," I suggested.

We sat at the top of the stairs and I took a deep breath.

"I'm really sorry about yesterday," I began.

"It's not your fault," she said, staring straight ahead. "I knew it wasn't a good idea for us to try to be friends and I let you talk me into it anyway."

"I still think we can be friends," I said. "I just think we need to set some boundaries."

She didn't answer. I think she'd already made up her mind, but I pressed on anyway.

"Lily told me we shouldn't touch each other, but I didn't listen to her."

"Lily?"

"My sister."

"I know who Lily is, but . . ."

"I . . . I've had a really hard time dealing with all this," I explained. "Lily's been helping me get through it."

Josette lowered her eyes.

"I'm sorry," she finally said.

"No," I replied, shaking my head. "You don't have anything to be sorry about. I'm not telling you this so you'll feel bad, but I've been really struggling for almost a year and . . ."

I hesitated.

"I don't want to lose you again, Josie," I said.

"We can't be around each other, Marco," she said emphatically. "We have feelings for each other that we're not supposed to have and we need to *stay away* from each other."

"I'm going to have feelings for you whether I'm around you or not."

She glanced at me again and then sighed, shaking her head as she looked away.

"I *am*, Josie," I said. "I'm sorry, but I'm just trying to be honest. Keeping away from you isn't going to change that . . . as a matter of fact, if I don't see you I'm probably going to think about you even more because I'm going to be worried about you all the time. At least this way I can make sure you're okay."

She sighed again.

"I'm not saying it's okay for us to think about each other like . . . we used to," I said, "but I think it's okay if we just think about each other as friends."

"And how are we supposed to do that?"

"My mom always said that you can't stop birds from flying over your head, but that doesn't mean you need to let them build a nest in your hair."

"*What?*"

"You can't stop things from coming into your head," I clarified, "but that doesn't mean that you need to let them stay there."

She looked at me doubtfully, but I knew she was considering what I was saying.

"I think we can be friends," I said again, "if we just set some clear boundaries."

"Like no touching?" she asked dryly.

"That's one of them." I nodded seriously. "And not letting ourselves think about . . . well, about things we shouldn't be thinking about."

She didn't respond. I decided to keep going.

180

"And you need to start going back to church with me," I said.

This made her look at me in surprise.

"I can't," she said instantly, shaking her head. "I can't go back there and face all those people like this." She put her hands on her belly.

"What people?" I asked, almost with a laugh. "All those old people who think the world revolves around you?"

She bit her lip.

"They *love* you, Josie," I insisted. "They ask about you all the time and they would love to see you and they wouldn't judge you. And even if they did, you don't have anything to be ashamed of."

She looked down at her feet.

"What else?" she finally asked.

I hesitated.

"God wants us to be praying for Stuart," I said.

That *really* made her look at me in surprise.

"I know that probably sounds weird coming from me," I admitted, "but all God wants is for each of us to be closer to Him. You, me . . . even Stuart."

Of course I had balked when God told me that He wanted me to pray for Stuart, but He'd kept at me.

God wants all *people to be saved and to come to a knowledge of the truth.*

It really was that simple, and through His grace, God showed me that it was my job to pray that He would work in each of our lives to bring us closer to Him. I wasn't supposed to worry about *how* it happened . . .

I was just supposed to pray that it did.

"I don't know how God's going to bring Stuart closer to Him," I told her. "It might be through you or it might be some other way. I don't know."

She looked at me earnestly as I continued.

"But I do know that it's what He wants, and praying for that to happen is what we're supposed to do . . . or at least it's what *I'm* supposed to do."

She continued to stare at me.

"What do you think?" I asked after a moment. "Are you with me?"

She thought for another moment, and then she slowly nodded her head.

~ ~ ~

WITH THIS NEW focus – one that was right – things were easier. Josette and I quickly settled into a new routine that was remarkably similar to the one we'd been in while we were dating (minus all the hugging and kissing).

Josette came over to my house for dinner almost every evening.

We watched *Chances Are* while we ate.

We only broke our "no touching" rule once.

It was when Josette was about twenty-eight weeks along.

We were at my place, sitting quite apart from one another on the couch watching our show, when all of a sudden – right in the middle of a question – Josette let out a cry of surprise and put her hand to her belly. I looked at her curiously.

"She just *really* kicked!" she said, glancing at me. We knew she was having a girl . . . Stuart and Josette had decided to name her Sophie.

I didn't say anything, but then she said, "There she goes again."

I looked at her for a long moment, and she looked at me, and then Josette slowly moved her hand.

I turned my eyes to her rounded abdomen and moved closer, reaching my own hand out until I touched her belly. Almost immediately I felt a little kick, and then another stronger one.

I looked back at Josette.

She just stared at me quietly, not saying a word. I kept looking at her as her baby continued to kick, and then slowly, I lowered my head and I rested it against her pregnant belly. I stared at Josette for another long moment. Then I closed my eyes.

And I lay there against her like that for a long time, feeling her little girl move beneath me.

I prayed for her. I prayed to God that Sophie would be a perfect little baby who had all her fingers and all her toes and perfect lips. I prayed for her mommy.

And I prayed for her daddy.

Sophie continued to move underneath me, punching her little fists and kicking her little legs. I pressed my head tighter against her while I prayed, and when I was finished I turned my head and gave her a kiss through all of her mother's clothes and skin.

It was the most intimate moment I had shared with anyone in my life.

~ ~ ~

PRAYING FOR STUART wound up being a lot easier to do than I thought it would be. It was actually pretty simple.

How, after all, could I not want someone to grow closer to God?

Of course sometimes my mind would go where it shouldn't go . . . sometimes I would worry about exactly *how* God was going to work it all out. On every level I was still hoping that Josette and Stuart were going to get divorced – it was all I could do to not count down the days. Usually, however, I was able to force myself to get back to praying for the end result and not worry about the means.

But not always.

One day, as my mind wandered to thoughts of a future in which Josette and Stuart got back together and I would never see her again, I was surprised to discover that my first concern was not that Josette wouldn't be in my life anymore, but that I would never get to find out what God did in Stuart's life . . .

I'm pretty sure the fact that I worried about that first was another step.

Josette was due at the end of October, and she hoped that the baby wouldn't come until after she took her exams. She would then be able to stay home with Sophie until classes started at the end of January before putting her in daycare. Josette was determined not to miss any school: she said that if she quit now, she'd never go back.

For the most part, her pregnancy progressed uneventfully, but one morning – in early August – my phone woke me before five. I knew before I picked it up that it was Josette and that something was wrong, I turned on the light and started looking for my car keys before I even answered it.

"I'm sorry to bother you," were the first words out of her mouth.

"What's wrong?"

"I . . . I'm bleeding a little bit and I haven't felt her move in a long time."

"Did you call the doctor?"

"Yes."

"What did she say?"

"She wants to meet me at the hospital," Josette said, "but Stuart isn't answering his phone and . . ."

She hesitated.

"I'm sorry to bother you," she said again. "But is there any way you could come get me?"

"I'm already on my way," I said, and I started the car.

I helped Josette check in at the hospital, but then I stayed in the waiting room after she was taken back to see the doctor. I sat in a plastic chair with my elbows on my knees and my forehead resting against my hands. I'd been sitting there like that for a long time when I heard someone at the check-in window ask for Josette.

I looked up and saw a man standing at the desk and I knew instantly that it was Stuart. I watched as he was directed down the hall where Josette had been taken and then – when he disappeared from sight – I put my head back in my hands.

It was more than an hour before Josette and Stuart came back out into the waiting room.

I was prepared to not make eye contact . . . to look away and act as if I had never seen Josette before in my life if that's the way she wanted to play it, but she walked right up to me and introduced me to Stuart.

"Stuart," she said, "this is Marco. Marco, this is Stuart."

I stood up and extended my hand.

"Hi," he said as he shook it. He didn't flinch.

"Marco used to be my landlord," Josette explained. "He drove me here this morning."

Landlord.

"Thanks, mate," Stuart said, shaking my hand again. "My phone was on vibrate and I left it out in the living room. I usually try to keep it next to me at night."

I nodded and looked at Josette worriedly.

"She's fine," Josette said, putting a hand on her belly. "They did an ultrasound and she's great and the bleeding stopped. It wasn't very much, and they said unless it starts back up again it was probably nothing."

"And we're already at thirty-four weeks," Stuart added, putting a hand on the small of Josette's back. "I mean obviously they want her to hang in there a little bit longer than this, but if they need take her now or whatever she'll be fine."

I sighed in relief. Stuart put his other hand on Josette's belly and patted it in a reassuring way.

I looked at Josette.

"Do you . . . uhhh . . . do you need a ride back?" I asked.

"Oh, no," Stuart said. "I've got it." He reached out to shake my hand one more time. "Thanks for helping out."

I nodded at him.

"Thank you," Josette echoed softly, and the two of them turned together and headed out the door.

The next time I saw Stuart was also in a waiting room at the hospital. Brenda called me one morning while I was driving to the university to let me know that Josette was in labor and had asked her to call me. Brenda was there when I arrived, and the two of us sat in relative quiet while we waited for some kind of word from the birthing room. We were there for about two hours before Sophie was born, crying so loud that we could hear her in the waiting room.

Eventually the crying stopped and soon a nurse wheeled a little bassinet past us. Not too long after that, Stuart came out, headed in the same direction as the bassinet. As he passed by, however, he spotted us and immediately stepped into the room.

"Hi," he smiled, walking over to me. He reached out to shake my hand once again. "You're Marcus, right?"

"Marco," I corrected.

"Right, right," he said. "Sorry." He turned to Brenda. "And you must be Brenda?"

She nodded and congratulated him.

"Thanks," he grinned. "You wanna see her? They took her down here to poke and prod her a bit."

We followed Stuart down the hall until we came to a viewing area where a nurse was busy making little Sophie very angry.

Stuart touched the glass and looked at his daughter, talking to us as he smiled. "She's got a good set of lungs, eh?"

Brenda and I both agreed that she did.

He kept his eyes on her for a long time, and then he said quietly, almost to himself, "I can hardly believe how much she looks like Jamie."

Josette had nurses and doctors and a husband to take care of everything, and she really didn't need any friends hanging around. Long after Brenda went home, however, I found myself still at the hospital, unable to tear myself away. Sometime in the evening, I went to the cafeteria to get some dinner. I was sitting in a booth by myself, eating, when Stuart happened by carrying his own tray of food.

"Hi," he said, giving me a smile when he spotted me. "How's it going?"

"Good."

"Good," he nodded. "Want some company?"

"Sure."

He sat down opposite me and started tearing open packets of ketchup.

"My mom and dad are flying in tonight," he went on. "I've got to go pick them up at the airport in about an hour."

I nodded.

"Josie's sleeping," he added.

I nodded again.

"So you were Josie's landlord?" he asked, dunking a fry into his ketchup.

"Yeah," I said. "Before, when she . . ."

I wasn't sure how to word it, but Stuart didn't seem to need any further explanation.

"We're friends now," I finished with a shrug.

He nodded at me and took a bite of his burger.

"You wanna see something?" he asked.

"Sure."

He pulled out his phone and punched away at it for a moment. When he found what he was looking for, he held it up before me.

"That's Jamie," he said. "The day she was born. Doesn't Sophie look just like her?"

I had to nod again.

He shook his head as if he could still hardly believe the resemblance.

"I think Josie's kind of having a hard time with it," he added quietly. "It brings back a lot of memories."

I didn't say anything.

"Look," he went on, holding his phone out to me. "This is the last picture we ever took of her."

It was Jamie at Fitzroy Gardens, standing in front of the Fairies Tree.

"She was beautiful," I said.

"Thanks," he said.

He took a bite of his burger. After he had finished chewing, he swallowed. He looked at me for a moment and then asked, "Did Josie tell you that Sophie's going to have a little brother in a few weeks?"

I nodded and he continued to look at me quietly for a moment.

"You probably think I'm terrible," he finally said.

"No," I said. I shook my head.

He didn't say anything.

"I think you've been through something awful," I said, "and I think you're having a hard time dealing with it."

He seemed to think about that for a moment.

"Yeah," he said, giving me a little nod. "That's about right."

I hesitated for a moment, but then I said, "I want you to know that I've been praying for you."

He studied me for one more moment and then he nodded again and replied quietly, "Thanks."

I nodded back at him, and we both went back to our food.

At first, between Stuart and Stuart's parents, Josette had a lot of help when she went home from the hospital. But nine days after Sophie was born, Rebecca gave birth to Stuart's son, Mitch, and then a few days after that, Stuart's parents flew back to Perth. Suddenly Stuart's parents were gone, Stuart was extremely busy with Mitch and Rebecca, and Josette's dad and stepmom weren't planning a visit until March.

Things would have been hard for her anyway, but trying to keep Fran placated just about sent Josette over the edge. Fran stormed into her bedroom, slamming her door every time Sophie cried. She made it clear that the bags under her eyes were due to not being able to get a good night's sleep anymore. She dumped wet laundry from the washer straight onto the dirty floor if Josette didn't put it into the dryer quick enough. She sighed heavily if Josette dared to breastfeed Sophie in the living room.

Josette had bags under her eyes, too. She was already tired just from all the normal stuff that came with having a new baby, but trying to keep Fran happy took it to a whole new level.

Then, to top it all off, Josette started classes again at the end of January like she'd planned.

That's when things really went downhill.

I called Lily.

"Remember those pregnancy hormones you were telling me about?" I asked.

"What about them?"

"Are they gone now?"

"Yeah."

"Are you sure?"

"Oh yeah," she said, "they're gone. She's not going to feel like having sex for about five years."

"Five years?"

"I'm kidding."

"But they really are gone?" I asked.

"Yes."

"Are you sure?"

"She just had a baby, Marco," Lily explained patiently. "She's exhausted."

"Yeah," I said. "Tell me about it."

Two weeks after classes started back up, I went over to Josette's apartment and climbed the stairs. I could hear Sophie crying before I even knocked.

"Let's take her for a ride," I suggested after Josette answered the door, looking disheveled. "Maybe it'll help her fall asleep."

"She's not the one who's having trouble sleeping," Josette pointed out. "*I'm* the one who's having trouble sleeping."

"Well maybe you'll fall asleep," I said with a smile. "Come on."

We loaded the baby into her carrier and fastened her into the back seat.

"Where are we going?" Josette asked.

"I was thinking Yarra," I shrugged, "but if you want to do something else . . ."

"Yarra's fine," she said wearily.

We talked a little bit as we headed toward Yarra Boulevard, but for the most part, we were quiet. Sophie fell asleep quickly, and shortly after I turned onto the scenic drive, headed for Kew, Josette fell sound asleep, too.

That was fine with me. I just kept driving.

We had only been on the road for about twenty minutes though when Sophie woke up and started crying again.

"Where are we?" Josette asked, rubbing her eyes.

"Almost to Templestowe," I said.

"She can't be hungry again," Josette said, glancing toward the back seat. "She just ate an hour ago."

"Maybe her diaper needs to be changed."

"Maybe."

We reached Westerfolds Park and I turned into a parking area.

"Stay put," I instructed Josette. I got out, opened the back door, and started undoing buckles and straps.

"Did you make a mess?" I asked Sophie in a baby-talk voice.

I pulled her free from her car seat.

"You're lucky I have so many nieces," I said, laying her down on the back seat. "Messes are my specialty."

She stopped crying and looked at me as I undid the snaps on her outfit and checked her diaper. It was clean and dry.

"I think she was just lonely," I told Josette, fastening Sophie's diaper and clothing back up. I cradled her in my arms and stroked her cheek softly.

"Thank you," Josette said quietly from the front seat.

"No problem."

She sighed and rested her head back against the headrest, closing her eyes again.

"Josie?"

"Hmmm?"

"I want to talk with you about something," I said.

"What?" She opened her eyes and looked back at me suspiciously, obviously realizing for the first time that I hadn't taken her out just for some random ride.

"You can't keep going on like this," I said gently. "You're taking classes and working all day and then coming home and trying to study and take care of Sophie and worrying all the time about keeping her quiet so she doesn't wake Fran up at night and it's just too much. You're practically dead on your feet. You can't keep it up."

"I don't have much choice."

"Yes, you do."

"I'm not quitting school," she insisted, shaking her head.

"I'm not suggesting that you quit school—"

"And I'm not giving her to Stuart and Rebecca," she said, her voice rising.

"No," I agreed. "That's not what I was going to suggest either."

"What then?"

"I want to help you."

"You already are helping me."

"I mean more. I want to do more."

"Like what?"

I hesitated.

"I want you to move back in with me," I said.

"What?"

"I don't care if she wakes me up at night," I explained. "As a matter of fact, I can get up and feed her for you sometimes so that you can get more than three hours of sleep at a time, and I can pick her up from daycare so you don't have to drive over there during rush hour . . ."

She stared at me.

"I want to help you," I said again quietly, glancing down at Sophie. I shifted her slightly in my arms before looking up at Josette again. "Please let me help you."

She looked back at me for only another brief moment and then, to my surprise, she slowly nodded her head.

"Okay," she said quietly. "Thank you."

"Wow," I said, feeling my eyes widen in surprise. "I can't believe you just agreed to that. You must be *way* past exhausted."

"You have no idea," she replied, and she closed her eyes.

~ ~ ~

I KNEW THAT Josette and Sophie might not be with me long. There was more than a strong possibility that Stuart would want to get back together with Josette – in fact, I felt it was almost a certainty.

Threat of major change seemed to be what made Stuart take action.

From what I could figure, he had gotten back together with Josette only when faced with the reality that their divorce was almost final.

He'd started things back up with Rebecca, with Josette unaware, as soon as he found out he was going to be a father again.

He had left Josette a second time once he'd realized that Rebecca was pregnant, too.

Now that divorce from Josette was imminent once more, I braced myself for what he might do.

I didn't know the exact date.

I didn't ask.

But I was ready for whatever happened – or at least as ready as I could be.

I wasn't going to be blindsided again.

And I wasn't going to turn away from God this time . . . even if things didn't go my way.

~ ~ ~

THINGS WERE BETTER after Josette moved back in, but still far from perfect. Sophie stayed with her dad at least one night almost every weekend. Whenever we got her back on Sunday, Josette fretted and fumed about how Stuart and Rebecca had obviously given Sophie formula (even though she had pumped all week and made sure she'd sent plenty along), or about how they'd used diapers that gave her a rash, or about how Mitch had given her a cold.

As particular as she was about what she wanted for Sophie, however, and as adamant as she was that Stuart and Rebecca were *not* going to have primary custody, Josette remained surprisingly reserved around Sophie. She did all the right things: she took care of Sophie . . . she talked to her . . . she held her and kissed her . . .

But she never sang to her . . .

And she never smiled . . .

And there always seemed to be a distance between the two of them. I couldn't put my finger on it. I couldn't quite identify it. But it was there.

It was so strong that I could almost feel it.

I loved to sing to Sophie. By the time she was four months old, "Pop Goes the Weasel" would make her squeal with delight. After work I would pick Sophie up from daycare and then we would head home. I'd set her in her carrier on top of the little table in the kitchen so that she could watch me, and the two of us would make each other laugh while I worked on dinner.

One evening Josette came home just as I was lighting the grill. She took Sophie out of her carrier and the two of them disappeared into their bedroom for a while, reemerging just as I was pulling marinated lamb chops out of the fridge.

"Did you check the mail today?" Josette asked.

I thought for a minute.

"No," I said, shaking my head. "I forgot."

"My dad said he was sending her a book," Josette said, laying Sophie down on the couch. "I'll go see if it's there."

"I'll check," I said, waving my hand at her. "I'm going out to put the meat on anyway."

I threw the chops onto the grill and then went to the mailbox, flipping through the letters as I walked back toward the porch.

There was nothing large enough to contain a book, but one envelope in particular – addressed to Josette – made me stop in my tracks. I looked at it for a long minute and then climbed the stairs to go into the house.

I opened the door. Josette was standing in the living room, waiting for me. Maybe she was hoping the book had come, but I don't think so.

I think she knew.

I looked at her for a long moment and then handed her the letter. She stared at it as long as I had.

She didn't look at me, and she didn't open the letter. Instead, she walked past me to the door and pushed it closed. I turned around and watched as she stood at the door with her back to me, still staring at the unopened letter. Slowly she turned and leaned her back against the door, continuing to stare at the envelope in her hand.

Finally she opened it. She pulled out the paper inside and scanned it for a moment, leaning back against the door before lowering the letter to her side and looking up at me.

"I'm divorced," she said quietly.

I managed to nod at her.

And then she burst into tears.

In all the time I had known her – through everything she'd been through – I had never seen Josette cry.

196

Never.

Not even a single tear.

But now . . . now she was standing in front of me, sobbing?

I had absolutely no idea what to do.

"What's wrong?" I asked.

That just made her cry harder.

"Josette," I said, tentatively stepping closer. "It's okay, Josette. It's okay."

She just shook her head and sobbed. I stepped even closer and then reached out and put my hand on her arm. When she felt my touch she brought her hands up to cover her face, but she also let me move closer to her and she buried her head against my shoulder. I wrapped my arms around her and just held her while she wept.

"I'm sorry," she finally said after she'd cried for another minute.

"What's wrong?" I asked again quietly.

"I don't know," she sniffed. "I know this is what we've been waiting for and I know this is supposed to make me happy, but . . ."

She didn't finish.

"But what?" I asked gently.

She pulled back from me and looked into my eyes.

"I don't know if I'm ever going to be happy again," she said tearfully.

I searched her eyes.

"Why?"

"I . . . I don't know," she cried.

I continued to look at her.

"Did you want things to work out between you and Stuart?" I asked.

"No," she said honestly, shaking her head. "I mean . . . if that's what God wanted me to do then I was going to do it, but . . ."

"Are you worried that he's going to try to get Sophie now?"

"No," she replied, shaking her head again. "I don't think he'd do that."

I thought for a moment, and then I asked her gently, "Do you think you're scared that if you let yourself be happy you're going to lose everything again?"

She didn't even have to think about that. She immediately started sobbing again, nodding her head and burying it back against my shoulder.

I just held her and stroked her hair while she cried. After another few moments she finally quieted down enough to talk again.

"I'm scared to love her," she said tearfully, taking a deep, quavering breath and pulling away from me so that she could glance at Sophie. Then she looked at me. "I'm scared to love you . . ."

"You're not going to lose either one of us," I promised, shaking my head.

"You don't know that," she cried, her voice rising in alarm. She pulled even further away now, searching my eyes and shaking her head. "You can't say something like that. You don't have any idea what's going to happen in the future."

I didn't answer for a moment.

"You're right," I finally admitted quietly. "I don't know what's going to happen."

She looked at me grimly.

"And I get scared too," I said. "I worry that maybe God's going to want something different than what I want, but you can't let fear keep you from enjoying your life, Josie. How many times does the Bible tell us *not* to fear?"

"I know it does," she said, "and I'm *trying*, but–"

"No, you're not," I interrupted. "You're not trying at all."

She looked at me in surprise.

"You're not, Josie," I said. "You're . . ."

I closed my eyes, letting out a deep breath and shaking my head. I opened them again and looked at her earnestly, making sure she was really listening to what I was about to say.

"You're . . . you're amazing," I finally said gently. I touched the side of her face before I went on. "I've never known *anybody* who could go through all the things you've gone through and still hold on to their faith the way that you have. You always put

God first and you're willing to give up whatever you want in order to do what you think He wants . . ."

She looked up at me solemnly.

"You're like the poster child for what we're supposed to do when bad things happen . . ." I hesitated. "But you *suck* at how we're supposed to act when good things happen."

Her mouth dropped open in protest.

"You do, Josie!" I insisted before she could say anything. "God *loves* you and He wants you to be *happy*. You're never happy anymore."

"He doesn't tell us that He wants us to be happy," she argued. "Nowhere in the Bible does it tell us that we're going to be *happy*!"

"It tells us to rejoice!" I argued right back. "Over and over and over again. How many times does it tell us to rejoice?"

She didn't answer.

"We're supposed to rejoice," I said quietly. "And we're supposed to be *thankful*."

"I am," she said weakly.

"No, you're not," I said, shaking my head.

She looked back at me quietly and I searched her eyes.

"When was the last time you were joyful about anything?" I asked.

Once again, she didn't answer.

"The last time I remember," I went on, "was about a year and a half ago."

I pointed to the couch.

"Right over there," I said. "Remember?"

Her eyes dropped to the floor again and I knew that she remembered.

"I think it was the last time I heard you laugh," I told her.

I reached under her chin and lifted her face until she was looking at me again. We stared at each other in silence.

"Look what's on that couch right now," I whispered, nodding my head toward Sophie.

Josette's eyes filled with fresh tears as she looked at her daughter.

"She is a *gift* to you from God," I said. "He loves you and He's given you this wonderful gift and He expects you to be *thankful* for it and He expects you to be *joyful* about it."

A tear rolled down her face and she looked back at me.

"She needs you, Josie," I whispered. I wiped the tear away and looked closely at her for a very long moment. "*I* need you."

She closed her eyes and another tear fell. I brushed that one away too, and then I slowly leaned toward her and kissed her cheek where it had been.

I heard her take in a sharp breath.

"I love you," I whispered, and I kissed her again.

Slowly she exhaled and I moved my lips along her skin, caressing her neck and kissing where her salty tears had been.

She grabbed for my hand and squeezed it, letting out a soft moan as I worked my way back up her throat until I found her lips. She reached her other hand to the back of my neck and pulled me closer as she kissed me back, and I moved toward her, pressing her body against the door with mine. It seemed like we kissed for an eternity, but it was nowhere near long enough.

"I have missed you *so* much," I breathed when we stopped long enough for me to talk.

"I've been right here the whole time," she said, looking at me with the slightest trace of a smile on her face.

"No," I answered seriously, shaking my head. "No."

"Well . . . I'm here now."

I laid my hand alongside her face and held her gaze.

"I love you," I whispered again.

"I love you, too," she whispered back.

I looked at her.

"That's the first time you've ever told me that," I said.

She looked back at me uncertainly.

"It is," I insisted. "I've said it to you about twenty times but you've never said it back to me."

"I'm sorry," she said ruefully.

"It's okay," I assured her with a smile. "You can make it up to me."

"Oh, really?" she asked, a glint in her eyes now. "And how am I going to do that?"

I only hesitated a moment before answering.

"Marry me."

She looked at me in surprise.

"I'm serious, Josie," I said quietly. "I know you just got divorced, but I don't want to wait. I want to marry you right now, and I want to spend every day of the rest of my life with you and I want to be there for you and I want to be there for Sophie and I want to give her lots of brothers and sisters and I want to fall asleep with you in my arms every night and wake up next to you in the morning . . ."

I waited for her reply.

She looked at me worriedly.

"It's not going to be easy," she said, casting another glance toward Sophie. "Stuart and Rebecca are going to be a part of our lives for the next eighteen years."

"That's not necessarily a bad thing," I said, shaking my head. I had the strangest urge to smile.

"They aren't going to do things the same way we do," she said anxiously. "We're going to have to battle them about what time she should go to bed and what movies she gets to watch and who she gets to hang out with after school.

"And Sophie's already going to have one brother that she only gets to see part of the time," Josette continued, talking faster. "And if we have kids—"

"*When* we have kids," I interrupted.

"*When* we have kids," she corrected, "she's going to wonder why she's the only one who has to go back and forth all the time and why she can't just live in one place like they do . . ."

Her voice trailed off.

"And I just . . ." She dropped her eyes to the floor. "I just think you need to know that it's not going to be easy," she finished quietly.

I cupped my hand under her chin and tilted her beautiful face toward mine.

"I never said I wanted *easy*," I smiled, bending my head toward hers. I found her lips and kissed her again before pulling away just long enough to whisper, "What I want is *you*."

~ ~ ~

The End

~ ~ ~

Thank you so much for sharing Marco's story with me! Please take a moment to leave a review when you have a chance and be sure to keep up with the latest by joining the *Chop, Chop* page on Facebook at www.Facebook.com/ReadChopChop or visiting my blog at www.LNCronk.blogspot.com

The next companion novel to the *Chop, Chop* series is entitled *Taken*. No release date has been set yet, but on the next page you will find the description from the back cover and the prologue.

Taken
By L.N. Cronk

(From the Back Cover):

What if you fall in love with someone, but she's already taken?

What if she's your best friend's girlfriend?

If you're a good friend, you ignore the feelings that you're having. You forget the fact that she's everything you've ever wanted in another person . . . and things you didn't even know you wanted. You pretend that your heart doesn't race a little faster every time you see her. You act like you couldn't be more happy for your best friend.

That's what you do.

But what if your best friend suddenly disappears? What do you do then?

(Prologue):

Paul told me once that he wanted to be a martyr. I told him he was an idiot.

That happened a lot in the early years . . . when we were young . . . before he disappeared. He would say something profound, and I would completely blow him off.

But if he wanted to tell me something now, I wouldn't blow him off . . . I would listen.

I'd listen to every single thing he had to say.

www.ingramcontent.com/pod-product-compliance
Lightning Source LLC
Chambersburg PA
CBHW070834120626
46556CB00002B/760